Hourglass Romance

ROMANTIC FLIGHTS OF FANCY

PAULLETT GOLDEN

& GUEST AUTHORS

Cover Design by Fiona Jayde Media
Interior Design by The Deliberate Page
Illustrations by Doan Trang
https://www.doantrangarts.com/

Also by Paullett Golden

This compilation is dedicated to all those who aspire. Whatever your dreams and ambitions, set the goal and take the steps to make it happen.

A Letter to the Reader

Dear Reader,

Within these pages, you'll find a collection of short fiction, eighteen stories, to be precise. Fourteen of these shorts are fan favorites previously published in the Romantic Encounters series — an annual anthology of one short novel plus twelve short fictions. Four of the shorts included in this collection are written by other authors, namely the contest winners of the Golden News flash fiction contest. While the fourteen fan favorites are historical, namely late 18th century and early 19th century, the four by other authors vary in time period, from Regency to contemporary. The winners featured in this collection range from debut authors to seasoned authors. Be sure to check out their bios at the end of the book to learn more about them and their works.

This collection is the first of the Romantic Flights of Fancy series. Each year, a new book will be released as part of this series, all permanently free in eBook format and printing cost only for paperback and hardback. The releases will alternate with even years being a collection of fan favorites from the Romantic Encounters series plus the inclusion of contest winning authors, and odd years being a collection of new and exclusive-to-series short stories plus the inclusion of contest winning authors.

A call for submissions will appear every year in the Golden News newsletter for those who would like to enter the contest for a chance to be published in the Romantic Flights of Fancy series. The contest is open to newsletter subscribers only. Note that the contest is for flash and short fiction only with era and romance subgenre at the discretion of the submitting author.

There are many types of flash fiction, ranging from micro fiction of only a few words to short fiction of a couple thousand. Within this anthology, you'll find pieces ranging from approximately three hundred words to three thousand. Each tale is a stand-alone story regardless of brevity.

You can look forward to a similar compilation of short fiction contest winners plus fan favs in future Romantic Flights of Fancy.

Enjoy!
Paullett Golden

Table of Contents

Hourglass Romance

Haunted

T hey said he bore the mark of the devil.

Poppycock, Rosalind thought.

Fools nattered in her ear — a castle shrouded in darkness, ghouls lurking, a master who ate the hearts of babes. *Utter rubbish*. Granted, the circumstances were unusual, but there was undoubtedly a rational explanation for the earl's behavior.

Every year, the flame of fear was fanned by the Earl of Tepes' exclusive house party on All Hallows' Eve. The earl himself invited — nay, challenged — thirteen unmarried ladies and their chaperones to dine at the castle. The lady who lasted an entire night would meet the earl as a potential bride. As of yet, no one had stayed until morning.

No one had seen the earl, either. Plenty claimed to have, each with horrific tales as unlikely as the next.

Never in Rosalind's dreams would she have considered accepting an invitation to such a silly contest, but life found her in desperate straits. Her uncle, despite his wealth, considered her a burden. Unmarriageable, long in the tooth, and headstrong, she would find herself with packed bags in hand before next month ended. In comparison, marriage to the "monstrous" Lord Tepes sounded divine.

Surveying her companions, Rosalind felt notably out of place. Each had a proper chaperone, whether their mother, elder sister, or aunt. She, however, had a disgruntled maid. Not that it mattered. The ladies sharing this carriage, and likely the others following, would not last long, all afraid of their own shadow. Not Rosalind. There were no such things as ghosts or spooks that went bump in the night.

A glance out the window did little to bolster her confidence, however. The castle rose above a low-lying fog, an overgrown garden stretching the length of the drive.

Carriages queued before a portcullis with latticed iron spikes. *Cheery.*

Departing safety one trembling foot at a time, the ladies and their chaperones watched agape as a one-armed footman turned the lever to raise the gate. The butler, stooped by a shoulder hump, shuffled towards them.

"Good evening," he said, one lazy eye roaming. "If you'll follow me, please."

The other ladies exchanged wary glances. Rosalind rolled her eyes and took the lead behind the perfectly amiable butler.

Twenty pairs of eyes watched them from mounted portraits, each with a gaze that followed the group from foyer to drawing room. One young lady whimpered. *Linear perspective*, Rosalind scoffed.

Garnet damask curtains shielded the windows. Candles illuminated the room. Shadows danced across brocade wallpaper—crimson with gilded acanthus leaves. A chill tremored skin despite the fire and warming wine. With no sign of host or ghost, the guests speculated what horrors awaited them this night.

An hour they waited until the hunched butler shambled them into the dining room, which glittered and glowed from candles extraordinaire. Decadent plates appeared with a *saut de basque* dance of footmen. Rosalind hid a smile. She could accustom herself to such a life.

A scream ripped through the room.

All heads turned to the youngest lady, a hand to her mouth, her gaze riveted on a blushing footman. Ah, *not* blushing. A pink face puckered with burn scars looked back at the young lady with such sorrow, Rosalind's heart bled for him. Ducking his head, the footman left the room, as did the girl and her mother shortly thereafter.

And then there were twelve.

Two courses served, the entourage relaxed to discuss the latest fashions in bonnets. Through such barren conversation, Rosalind eyed the room and footmen, the former opulent, the latter damaged. *Curious.*

Entertainment accompanied the third course.

It began with a *thump* and *scrape* above them. *Thump, scrape. Thump, scrape.* The sounds traveled across the ceiling. All eyes turned upwards. Downward it followed the wall, then scratched the length of the room, sending a girl into a swoon. No sooner did her aunt grab the smelling salts than a banshee screech shattered the air.

Four pairs of guests fled the castle with the devil on their heels, their dinners unfinished.

"Oh, for heaven's sake," Rosalind said to her remaining companions. "It was only a fox."

From side to side the guests eyed each other, wary. Only one of the sounds had been explained.

Eight contestants and their protectors finished dinner and returned to the drawing room for the delights of two brave girls' musical talents. One sang. One played. Unfortunately, the soprano resembled the strings of a violin in the hands of a novice. The neighboring werewolf felt as deafened as Rosalind, for not ten bars into the song, a spine-chilling howl bayed into the night.

The accompanist pounded discordant keys and shrieked herself off the piano bench. The howl ushered three more guests and their mothers out of the castle.

"This is ridiculous. There are no wolves in England," Rosalind rationalized to her four rivals and their guardians.

"Then how do you explain the night-howler?" questioned a matron whose eyes were as beady as her ward's.

"Well…perhaps…" She tapped her index finger to her mouth. "One of the footmen stubbed his toe on a table. Wouldn't you howl at such pain?"

The matron's expression soured.

A haughty girl, sitting unnecessarily far from the group, lowered her nose long enough to say, "Don't think he'll marry you even if you win the contest. No one wants a spinster for their countess."

So, the talons were unleashed at last. And they called the earl a monster?

Rosalind smiled. "I take it you're already planning your nuptials with our vampiric host."

"You can't frighten me," said the harpy. "I don't believe a word of such rumors. He, like so many men, wishes to avoid marriage. This is all a lark."

Brows arched, Rosalind stood. "Then I'm no competition for you. If you'll all excuse me, I wish to retire early. Good night."

Ignoring the harrumphs, she headed for the door. Two of the pairings joined her for an early rest. No sooner did the group reach the foot of the stairs than behind them erupted screams and footfalls. Lady Haughty and another contestant raced through the foyer to the front door, leaving cries of singing ghosts in their wake.

And then there were three.

For how long Rosalind lay in bed staring at the muralled ceiling, she could not say. She counted by sounds rather than by time. Another fox. Another howl. A curious dragging sound punctuated by thumps. If they had not arrived at the castle determined to last an evening without losing their soul to the beasts lurking in the shadows, no one would have been bothered by the peculiar combination of noises.

The staff were a curiosity, certainly. Victims of a monster? Unlikely. The host merely had a penchant for hiring the unwanted. That fact made him admirable.

Ah, a new sound. A giggle in the wall behind her bed, as though from a child hiding. Straining, she listened. The giggling moved along the wall. Was this the drawing room ghost?

A bang shook the paintings. Rosalind leapt out of bed, clutching her dressing gown. Ghoulish moaning ensued. The wall shuddered, the moans intensifying.

After lighting her bedside candle, a fumbling challenge in the dark, she donned a robe and made for the door.

Peering into the hallway, she saw only emptiness. Until the two doors down from hers opened to the flying nightgowns of the last guests and their relations, leaving Rosalind alone in the house except, of course, for her maid, though she had not seen the girl since undressing for bed.

Ears perked, she listened for the ghostly sounds. Silence.

With a shrug, Rosalind bowed her head back into her room, but not before catching a flash of color. Peeking once more around the door, she grinned. An earthly maid and footman crept out of a closet together, the footman adjusting his fall flap. Haunted castle, indeed.

Thump, rattle. Thump, rattle.

Eyes wide, Rosalind looked the opposite direction down the hall. Empty.

Thump, rattle.

Courage in her throat, she followed the sound. *Thump, rattle.* It came from behind the wall. Fingers strangling her chamberstick, she pressed an ear to the wood. *Thump, rattle, scrape. Thump, rattle, scrape.*

She rapped smartly on the wall. The sound paused before continuing around the corner into the gallery. She followed. Abruptly, it stopped again, pivoted, and went the opposite direction.

Had she not first heard a door open, she would not have been swift enough to douse her candle and duck behind a decorative bust. As it happened, she did hear a door. The peculiar part was there were no doors in the hall. Eyes straining in the darkness, she watched.

As though walking through the wall, a frail man appeared in the gallery, tray in hand. He took five steps to the opposite wall and disappeared again. Even that was not as notable as the clubbed foot he dragged and the rattling cutlery on his tray. Rosalind barely suppressed her mirth. Ghosts in the wall, indeed.

The footman thumped his way inside the opposite wall, leaving an empty hall behind him. Retracing his steps, she studied his exit point. It seemed ordinary enough. She pushed against the wood, feeling the grain for a seam or lever or something.

Click.

The wall angled and slid, a handy pocket door. A quick glance beyond revealed a well-lit servant's hallway. Sconces decorated the walls every few feet. To the right, the hall continued, and to the left it ended at a set of spiral steps. To the left she went. On second thought... She dashed back to set the candlestick by the door to mark the exit.

While uneven and narrow, the stairs climbed only one story before ending at an arched wooden door. Lifting the iron ring, she pushed open the door and stepped inside.

Before her was an inviting tower library. A fire roared in the hearth. The smell of leather-bound books enticed her. Though not a large space, it was warm and cozy. Lounging in front of the fireplace was the night-howler — a sizable bloodhound, its head on its paws. Facing the fire, its back to the door, was a winged chair.

Thunk, click.

The door shut behind her.

The bloodhound moved first, lifting its head to investigate. He thumped his tail and climbed to his feet to lumber to her. Rosalind calmed her beating heart by petting the bloodhound, whose baying bark had become a familiar sound that evening.

"About time you arrived," the voice from the chair growled. "I'm ravenous."

"Good heavens, do you mean to eat me?"

The beast was on his feet in a flash, hand braced against the mantel, teeth bared.

With his back to the firelight, his face hid in shadow. From all else she could see, he appeared a normal man. No, normal would be a disservice. He was a physically thrilling man with long black hair worn loose around broad shoulders, a hard chest visible in the vee of a starched shirt, and muscular thighs framed with buckskin breeches.

Her eyes roamed over his deliciously attractive physique in its state of half-dress. *This* was the monster? Had her stomach not fluttered so fiercely nor her cheeks warmed so feverishly, she would have laughed.

"I hadn't realized my butler would bring dessert before dinner," he said at last, recovering from the unexpected intrusion.

Her body flamed from his implication. Under normal circumstances, she would have thought of a witty retort. Alas, all she could do now was pet the dog.

"Haven't you heard, my lady? I eat virgins." He growled again, the effect lost when the bloodhound thumped his tail and trotted over to his master to nuzzle a pale hand.

Sucking in her breath, hand on her stomach, she said, "Well, I suppose that gives us both something to look forward to. I do believe that's a benefit of marriage, yes?"

Lord Tepes barked a laugh. For a moment, all tension was eased. But his laugh ended sharply.

"What are you doing in my study?"

She took a brave step forward. "Looking for a husband."

In the silence that stretched, she could feel the earl's gaze sweep over her. The sensation quickened her pulse.

Pushing himself away from the mantel, her host strode across the room, stopping mere feet away, and turned to catch the firelight on his features.

"Be careful what you wish for on All Hallows' Eve."

Tentative, nervous, excited, she approached to better look at him, a smile on her lips.

One blue eye and one brown watched her with intensity. A long streak of white laced the raven hair from temple to tip. Starting at the temple and stretching down to a clenched jaw was colorless linen-white skin.

And so, this was the devil's mark. Her smile broadened. He looked to her to be kissed by an angel.

He crossed his arms over his chest. "Now that you've seen behind the curtain, shall I arrange for a carriage?"

She reached a hand to touch his forearm, the skin hot through his shirtsleeve.

When he flinched at the touch, she said, "On the contrary. I'll sleep soundly this evening, if not smugly. You see, Lord Tepes, I don't believe in ghosts. I do, however, believe you owe me breakfast."

His expression relaxed into the semblance of a grin. "If I don't frighten you, then what of my staff?"

"People who have met with unfortunate circumstances. Certainly not goblins or ghouls." Taking a step closer, she reached a hand to the discolored cheek. "What I don't understand is the contest."

He stood still, allowing her to touch his face and hair, seemingly unaware of how erotic she found the fingertip exploration.

"I protect the unwanted and deformed as I protect myself. The contest perpetuates rumors and discourages callers. However much I might have hoped someone like you would last the night, I never expected it. For too long, I've been ridiculed and afraid, just as my staff. Now, we can do the laughing and cause the fear."

"You could make friends, you know, rather than hiding."

"You who are so perfect know nothing of society's cruelty. I've tried making *friends*. At one time, I thought my inheritance would be freeing. I was ready to start a new life as a peer, not an oddity. They took one look at me and turned away in horror. Perhaps with a countess—"

Standing on her tiptoes, Rosalind kissed the pale skin, her lips brushing his hot flesh.

In a breathless movement, she was pinned against the door, his lips pressed to hers, a kiss more passionate than she dreamt possible. Her arms wrapped around his neck, his hands exploring her waist through the dressing robe.

Lost in the kiss, she nearly missed the whimpering of the bloodhound. Reluctantly, their lips parted. Turning in unison, they spotted the pup staring at a far wall.

"One of your footmen must be carrying biscuits," she said with a laugh.

Brows furrowed, he said, "There's not a servant's hall behind that wall."

The dog ran in a circle and howled as an apparition floated through the wall, across the room, and into the adjacent wall, humming to herself.

Lord Tepes tightened his hold on Rosalind, as though expecting her to flee after all.

"I'm sure there's a logical explanation," she said, tilting her face in invitation.

He chuckled, his lips returning to their rightful place against hers.

Beguiled

T he anonymous letters first appeared in the news-
paper on February 1st and caused such a stir, she
hid at home for a week. No one doubted they
were written for her. How many Lady Ts of Shrop-
shire were there, after all?

The latest letter, featured in the Valentine's edition,
was the most scandalous:

> To the bewitching Lady T. of Shropshire:
> Thine eyes be green and thine hair red.
> Please, accept me so we may wed.
> I loved you at first sight
> And hope you don't take fright
> When you lay your precious eyes on me.
> Tonight, at last light, together we'll be.

The ball began at dusk.

Her dance card filled before she'd reached the
receiving line to greet her hostess. The eager faces of
bachelors all claimed with their waggling eyebrows to
be her secret admirer. Would he make himself known
tonight? *Would* she run in fright?

Though no one spoke to her, all eyes found her
from behind fans and hands.

Between the twirls and promenades of each dance, she scanned the crowd for clues. Whispers followed her, taunting her with tales of a clandestine romance.

And then she saw him.

A shadowed figure watched her from behind a potted plant. Her pulse raced, a roar in her ears masking the voices around her.

Their eyes met, and her world tilted. Hazel eyes peered at her from beneath heavy lids framed with dark eyelashes. Those eyes seemed to read her soul. Never had she believed in love at first sight. Until now.

He took a step towards her.

She stepped towards him.

A din of voices resounded around her, crescendoing when he took another step.

And then a clink of glass, drawing the attention of all in the room.

"But a moment, please, but a moment. I have an announcement," voiced the hostess. "It is a propitious Valentine's ball, indeed, for I have the pleasure of announcing the betrothal of my eldest daughter to Lord Keyes."

Her eyes never left his, though he took five more steps forward. She counted. How many more until he reached her?

He stopped. Her breath caught. He wasn't walking towards her, but rather to the center of the ballroom. A young miss affecting well-practiced ennui took his arm.

How could this be? *He* was the betrothed Lord Keyes?

No! She'd only just discovered him. She'd only just found love.

Oblivious to the girl on his arm, he continued to stare at her, his eyes ablaze.

Before she made a cake of herself, she tore her gaze from his and escaped by way of the terrace doors. Grasping the railing outside, she filled her lungs with air, staring at the sun setting behind a copse of trees.

Footsteps sounded behind her. A gossiping matron or a vapid girl to tease her?

A rumble intoned, "Elope with me."

She whipped around to come face-to-face with Lord Keyes. They stood but an arm's reach from each other.

"I don't know you," she whispered.

"Yes, you do. You knew me at first sight, just as I knew you." His cologne enveloped her, enticing her to move closer. "Come away with me."

"But what of your betrothed?"

"Inconsequential. I want you, only you. Come with me. Gretna Green awaits." He held out his hand. "Will you be me Valentine bride?"

Her family's disapproving faces flashed before her eyes.

"Yes." She slipped her hand into his.

They fled the terrace, darting hand in hand across the park to the circle drive.

Swift words to a curious coachman and a bump and jostle later, they were on the road, bound for Scotland. Her stranger pulled her against his chest, his arms wrapping around her shoulders to shield her from doubt. He kissed her deeply, soulfully, conveying to her all the words they'd not yet said, affirming his heart mirrored what hers did for him.

At length, she leaned away, smiling, memorizing his face, reaching a hand to trace the scar that ran from his left ear to his chin.

"I've loved you since the second letter," she confessed.

A crease deepened between his brows. "Letter? What letter?"

She laughed at his coyness and kissed him brazenly.

Until it dawned—he hadn't returned the laugh.

The carriage continued to Scotland, his question echoing in her mind.

Candor

Lord Eagleton died on a Wednesday. The townspeople rejoiced.

Friday, they gathered at the inn over ale and pasties, plotting.

"We won't suffer another tyrant's rule!" shouted one man.

A din of voices rose in assent.

"How do we know the cousin will be different? Same blood runs through his veins!"

The people jeered.

As meetings go, many voiced an opinion, most agreed, and nothing was accomplished.

When Cami left for home, it was not yet dusk. She chose the woods that separated Eagleton Park from the village. She knew the route well, and her terrier, Ferguson, made an efficient enough protector from the highwaymen the deceased Lord Eagleton had employed to line his pockets. His bandits plundered the fanciest of conveyances while terrorizing the villagers. As Lord Eagleton had taken a hefty portion of the profits, the highwaymen knew immunity for their crimes. All crimes.

But Cami could hold her own. As a vicar's daughter, she was acquainted with sin and villainy.

Beneath the canopy of the forest, the world darkened. Her feet trod on his land, trespassing. She smirked and trod farther. Slats of light shone where the setting sun parted leaves. She inhaled the woody scents, Ferguson trotting at her heels, ears erect and nose sniffing, on the watch for trouble.

It found her in a succession of flashes.

Ferguson barking ferocious yips. The responding neigh of a horse. Black horse flesh rising before her eyes. The world tilting as she fell.

A blade to her throat.

She dared not move. Ferguson continued to bark, the sound muffled and distant. The horse pawed at the ground, unnerved by the terrier. Her eyes focused, time slowed to a normal pulse. Sabre in hand, a masked rider loomed over her.

A highwayman! Fear made flesh in the shape of a man.

Her breath suspended. Oh no, no, *no*. Erratic, her heart pounded.

"When did highwaymen trade pistols for witchery?" the man demanded.

Eyes wide, Cami mouthed her confusion.

Brown eyes studied her. "You must've bewitched the woods to take me by surprise. Nary a sound I heard from you or the pup. Is witchery your only weapon, or shall you also employ your beauty to wrest my gold?"

Ferguson moved between them and growled, prepared to defend his lady.

Finding her voice at the end of the sabre, she asked, "Are *you* not a highwayman?"

Gruff, he barked, "Do I *look* like a highwayman?"

A pointed glance found the blade. "You'll pardon me for saying, but at the present, you do."

With swift movement, the stranger sheathed the sword then removed his riding mask. He reached a hand to help her rise.

His face was too angular, his nose too hawkish, his eyes too dark to be handsome. Still Cami found herself breathless. Licking lips that had gone dry, she grimaced.

"My apologies," he said. "Are you injured? You've surprised me out of my manners, my lady."

"Mrs. Black, actually, and I'm uninjured." She made a show of shaking the dirt from her dress.

"Is Eagleton Park far, do you know?" As if to prove his good intentions, he kneeled before Ferguson and reached out a hand. The traitor of a terrier abandoned his bark, wagged a tail, and licked the palm.

"You're on the property now. The house is a mile west."

"You shouldn't walk the woods alone, Mrs. Black."

"Yes, well, it's not your concern. My home isn't far." She made to leave.

"You are my concern, Mrs. Black. Allow me to introduce myself." He sketched a bow. "Lord Eagleton. Newly inherited. I clean up well, I assure you. I shall see you safely home."

His smile twisted her stomach into knots. It remained so for their entire walk to her cottage.

He had such ideas! A new canal to prevent flooding. A raise in wages. Investment opportunities for the tenant farmers. Building improvements. He spoke sincerely, with an air of excitement. Was it all to be believed? His eyes spoke truth.

But the people had suffered too long under the former Lord Eagleton. They would never trust this new one.

Something bubbled in Cami's chest. A bold and daring idea.

"You need an ally," she said. "Someone of the people, someone they trust."

"Do I?" he asked, brows raised.

She ignored his skepticism. "Allow me to be that person."

"Why you?" His eyes searched her face.

"I've lived here all my life. I believe what you say, but for the others to believe, you'll need an ally. I'm the vicar's daughter and the rector's wife. You need me by your side."

"I hadn't realized I was in search of an advisor."

"Not an advisor, my lord. A wife." Her knees trembled beneath her petticoat, her words far bolder than she felt. "Wed me, and the people will trust you."

"And what do you suppose the rector will say?" he asked, kneeling again to rub Ferguson's belly.

"I'm widowed, my lord. He was my father's best friend. It was a convenient match…" *if a miserable one*. She chastised herself for the thought. He'd not been unkind.

"I see. And ours would be a match of love, or of convenience?"

She flushed, questioning now the wisdom of her impetuous proposal.

Rising smoothly, he said, "I'll give you my answer before week's end. For now, know me to be bewitched." With a touch to his hat, he leapt on his horse and cantered away.

Cami slept not a wink for a week. How could she have been so bold? She had proposed to a stranger! The new Lord Eagleton, no less. But how could she not? She was a good judge of character, and she knew he was a good man. She dared not deny the flutter in her heart.

The end of the week arrived with a town meeting, the new Lord Eagleton presiding.

"Put action to words! Words are empty!" they shouted at his ideas. "How can we trust you? You'll cheat us!"

When the meeting reached its unruliest, his lordship stood, holding up staying hands. "I promise to show you. I will not be a tyrant lording over you. I will work alongside you. Consider me one of you."

When he held a hand to her, their eyes meeting, Cami dreaded she may swoon.

"Allow me to introduce my betrothed."

Chin high, she stood and walked to the front of the room. Placing a gloved hand in his, she turned to the townspeople and smiled through her shock and disbelief.

Gasps mingled with sighs and applause. "He is to be one of us," whispered the room.

Love or convenience? she asked herself daily, weekly, monthly.

The first time he hosted a town meeting to encourage farmers to invest in a canal, she hoped it to be love. The first time she witnessed him stripped to his buckskins, bare-chested and sweaty, shoveling the new canal alongside the laborers, she wanted it to be love. The first time he gazed adoringly into the eyes of their first born, she knew it to be love. A love that grew from a moment of whimsy into a lifetime of respect and trust.

As Lord and Lady Eagleton danced under the stars at the sixth annual fête, the villagers looked on and knew themselves most fortunate for never could there be a more loving lord and lady, with children who played with those in the village, the lines of greatness blurred.

Most importantly, she knew herself to be loved when he touched the back of his fingers to her cheek and whispered his affection. "I was right to first mistake you for a highwayman, Lady Eagleton. You've stolen my heart."

Persephone

The lattice of the casement window segmented the amber world outside into the yellows and reds of autumn.

"It's done." Her father's voice, firm and controlled, threatened to discompose her. "The contract is signed.

Chin quivering, Sofie pursed her lips to save her dignity. She would not give him the satisfaction of seeing her cry.

"I should thank you," she whispered, commanding her voice not to shake. "Never again can you lord over me."

Tearing her gaze from the window, she met his hard eyes, curtsied, and left.

The haven of her room had been divested of her belongings. They had packed away her life. A final, lingering look was all she gave.

In the foyer waited her mother, the one person Sofie had hoped would fight on her behalf against an arranged marriage to a stranger.

"This is for the best, dear," Mother said instead in her sweet soprano. "Sir Nathaniel is to be elected Lord Mayor of London. It's a good match."

Sofie bowed her head and stared at her hands, willing them, too, not to shake. "Yes, I can see how beneficial it would be for Father."

She was nothing more than a bartering chip in the politics of men.

An hour later, she was tucked in a hired carriage with her maid. They headed south to meet her betrothed at an inn halfway to London. Once officially acquainted, she and the baronet would proceed together for the wedding and his election.

The carriage bumped along, lulling her maid into a deep slumber but jarring Sofie out of her protective shell. The heel of her palm wiped tears from her cold cheeks.

Three tiring days later, the carriage was within an afternoon's distance of *the* inn. The one where she would meet her prescribed life's mate. If only she could meet another man, her perfect man, and elope out from under the villain who had arranged a wife of good family for political gain.

A light drizzle pattered against the carriage window, blurring the scenery. Sofie had never traveled farther south than Durham. Would London be so very different? Was it truly the mouth of hell? She shuddered. Sinking into the collar of her pelisse and wrapping her arms about her, she leaned her forehead against the window and closed her eyes.

A jolt woke her. Darkness shrouded the carriage. Rain pounded.

Were they far from their destination? Her maid's face pressed against the window in search of salvation.

In a fractured moment, the carriage swayed, tossing Sofie on her side. The world slid, shook, tilted. A scream pierced the storm, ending with a thud as her maid was flung against the carriage wall. The vehicle toppled to the ground and slid across mud. Sofie clung to the leather strap, her body prone on the side of the coach, her face staring up at the door.

All around her, men shouted, and horses whinnied. Her maid lay unconscious. Sofie had to get them out. She reached up for the door and shook the handle. Struggle as she might, the door would not budge. She pushed; she pulled; she prayed.

The door flung outwards, wrenched out of her hands. Rain splashed in her face.

"Are you injured?" a baritone rumbled.

Wiping her eyes of droplets, she peered up into a shadowed face framed by soaked hair.

"Give me your hands," the darkness commanded.

"My maid. She's injured. Please, take her first," Sofie shouted above the din of the storm.

"I can more easily get to her if you're out of the way. Take my hand."

A powerful forearm hauled her to safety. Once he saw her to firm ground, he climbed back on the carriage to retrieve her maid.

Several men dashed about in the rain, working to free the horses from the overturned carriage. Far from the ditch, another carriage stood, unharmed, beckoning with dry security.

"Follow me," said their savior, striding ahead of her, the maid cradled in his arms.

He nestled her companion on the opposite bench and turned to Sofie. "My man will see you to the inn."

He looked at her for no longer than a moment, but eternity stretched under his gaze. Sofie shivered in her drenched pelisse. The blackness of night hid his face, but she felt his compassion. Would he be scandalized if she threw her arms around his neck and kissed him?

Only when the carriage lurched forward did she realize she had not uttered a word of thanks.

The inn was nicer than expected, a large and clean establishment. The innkeeper's wife saw Sofie to her room, had a temporary maid sent up, and promised to tend to her companion, who had thankfully come to with a single sniff of smelling salts. Their luggage waited, not lost in the mud.

Had Sir Nathaniel arrived yet? Would he send for her to dine with him or wait until tomorrow? Her maid had chosen a lovely dress for their first meeting, but Sofie could hardly think of that now. She was tired and chilled. A cup of tea was what she needed most.

In dry clothes but with damp hair, she found her way downstairs. The public room was crowded with travelers seeking shelter from the storm. She searched impatient faces for the innkeeper or his wife or — no, she would not admit that she came in hopes of seeing her evening's hero.

But who was she to deny fate?

A flash of movement stole her attention. Broad shoulders bearing a drenched, multi-caped greatcoat strode into the inn, soaked black hair fanning about a chiseled face.

He made for the private parlor. The door closed behind him, leaving her hesitant. But she only wanted to thank him. What harm could come from a quick word of gratitude? This would be her only opportunity.

One step. Then another. Her hand perched on the handle. *Breathe.*

She saw herself into the private room.

"Excuse me. I don't mean to intrude, but—" Sofie choked on her remaining words.

The parlor was empty except for the man beside the fire. The greatcoat had been tossed across a chair. The cravat, coat, and waistcoat had followed. Before her stood a man in nothing but boots, buckskins, and a nearly transparent shirt that clung to his torso in sinful ways.

His hands swept his hair away from his face as he turned to her, his expression one of shock mixed with anger.

"This parlor is reserved," he barked.

She hardly heard. Angled features, square jaw, cleft chin… Her breath hitched at the sight of the bare chest framed by the shirt's open vee, the tapered waist, and the muscled thighs.

"Oh, it's you," he said, interrupting her admiration. "My apologies. I had thought to have the parlor to myself until dinner." With a lunge, he snatched up the soaked waistcoat.

"No, I'm the one who owes you an apology. I shouldn't have barged in. I only wanted to thank you for helping us."

"Damsels in distress are my speciality," he said with a wink. "I had planned to invite you to dinner after your respite. Seeing that you're already here, would you care to join me?"

The side door to the parlor opened.

The innkeeper stepped in, his eyes on the tray he carried. "Coffee, sir. And I've sent our boy to your suite until your valet arri—" He halted, the tray meeting the table with a *thunk*.

His mouth gaped as he looked from Sofie to the half-dressed man and back again. Taking a step back, he bowed and mumbled his apologies.

"Thank you, Mr. Fremont. I trust you've taken good care of my wife's quarters?"

"Yes, yes, the very best, as you requested." The innkeeper exited as quickly as he entered, leaving them alone once more.

Her first horror was at being caught in a room alone with a half-dressed man. Her second was learning he already had a wife, here at the inn, no less.

Amidst her shock, the man laughed. "Was it arrogant of me to announce you as my wife?"

"Your wife? You mean, Mr. Fremont thought you meant *me*?"

"But of course." He crossed the room in quick strides, grabbed her by the shoulders, and kissed her. A dizzying, spine-tingling kiss, his warm, moist mouth pressed to hers.

When he released her, she grabbed at his chest to hold steady. *This.* This was what she wanted. Not an arranged marriage, but *this.*

He raised a hand to her cheek, caressing her with the backs of his fingers. "Now it's your turn to rescue me, my lady."

"I'm afraid I can't. I…you see…I'm already betrothed."

"Yes, you are. *To me.* Sir Nathaniel Gilbert." He leaned in, teasing lips brushing hers once more. "At your service."

Masquerade

M ist enshrouded the castle, a sea fret of cold gloom. Lady Evelyn tugged at the edges of her threadbare traveling cloak, chilled by more than the November air.

She had come to win the heart of the reclusive Viscount Marr. Her competition lined the drive. Ladies of various ages and statuses stepped out of carriages and entered the mouth of stone and iron.

Shivering, she accepted the footman's hand and exited her own carriage, her aunt in tow. It was her aunt's influence that had gifted Evelyn this chance. While no one wanted a destitute bride, Aunt Augusta held enough persuasion to ensure her niece at least received an invitation.

Together they followed the other guests to the drawing room.

Not long after, a tall gentleman in a nondescript graphite ensemble, spectacles perched on his nose and raven hair closely clipped, stepped into the room, signaling for silence.

"Welcome, venerable guests," he said, his voice a velvet tenor. "I am your host, Mr. Brice, solicitor. Your safe arrival on this auspicious evening bodes well for our plans to find Viscount Marr a bride."

Murmurs hummed.

"No need to swoon, ladies, for there is no secret as to why you've been invited. His lordship will choose his bride from among you. On the eve of the masquerade, seven days hence, she shall be named. A plethora of entertainment awaits your pleasure, beginning with a musicale this evening, a picnic on the morrow, fireworks at dusk, and more. Please, drink."

The partygoers tittered as footmen circled with trays of claret.

Women in jewels and revealing bodices decorated the room, their chaperones hovering. Each measured the other, sizing up their opponents. An equal number of gentlemen attended, their eyes feasting on the available flesh.

Staring into her untasted wine, Evelyn frowned. Even with the persistent presses of Aunt Augusta, she could not entice herself to court a stranger, and certainly not one she had yet to meet. Viscount Marr had not left his castle for two decades. He was rumored to be near death and in desperate need of an heir. His wealth knew no bounds.

She looked back to the solicitor, in a corner away from the guests. His long fingers tapped his wine glass, his gaze studying each person, astute.

He cut a fine figure, though it was the intelligence behind the spectacles she found enchanting. If her aunt were not present, Evelyn would have sought his company. Ah, but he would not welcome hers. A man of no name or fortune would have little to gain from a woman who had name but no fortune.

Mr. Brice turned, his eyes meeting hers. Breath hitched, she smiled. He tilted his head, as though confused by her attention. Only when he returned her smile did she exhale.

The day after, a chill Wednesday with a leaden sky, the guests gathered on the lawn for bowls and gossip. Evelyn slipped away. The evening before had been tedious enough, wasted in the company of panting gentlemen and women whose words dripped with venom in their pursuit to poison the opposition. All for naught since the viscount was not among their numbers. In fact, no one had seen him.

A folly overlooked the lawn, a temple of ruined stone and climbing vines. It afforded Evelyn the perfect view to watch the play of avarice. Folding her hands in her lap, she enjoyed from afar the theatrics of fluttering fans. If only she had brought paints and canvas.

"Striking vista, no?"

Mr. Brice leaned against the stone.

She stood, acknowledging his reverent bow.

With an adjustment to his spectacles, he approached. "The entertainment isn't to your liking?"

"The company, more like. Oh, how discourteous of me to say." She stuttered a laugh. The way he looked at her made her stomach flutter and her skin flush in sinful ways. "I've no wish to gossip or flirt. I'd much rather paint, actually. And you? As master of ceremonies, should you not be mingling, taking notes for the viscount?"

Mr. Brice's lips curved at the corners.

With a low chuckle that tingled her toes, he asked rhetorically, "You think me a spy for his lordship?" He winked, bringing her attention to eyes of golden hazel. "I've taken enough notes for one morning. Besides, no one wants the company of a humble solicitor."

She waved her hand to the bench. "Join me?"

His expression curious, he sat. She settled beside him, increasingly aware of his proximity, his leg inches from her own, his body warming hers without touching.

Time warped, in one moment concave, in the next convex. For how long they spoke, Evelyn could not say, but she knew she wanted to see Mr. Brice again. How inconvenient to fall for a solicitor of little means. Despite the age and mystery of the viscount, Lord Marr was the better catch to ensure her family did not face ruin and starvation.

When a rainy day later in the week trapped the guests indoors, the two met again. As the others speculated about the viscount's condition, some believing him infirm, others deformed, Evelyn slipped into the library with Mr. Brice.

After an exchange on the inspiring views of the north tower, Evelyn asked, "Have you been Lord Marr's solicitor for long?"

His smile slipped. "Since June."

"Do you enjoy the work?"

"It's… different. I've been a solicitor for ten years and love what I do, but it will take time to accustom myself to these surroundings." Crossing one lithe leg over the other, he steepled his fingers. "The presence of a Lady Marr will help."

Evelyn tucked a curl behind her ear, both thrilled and anxious at being alone with him.

"Why is he choosing a stranger as a bride? Does he not care whom he marries?" If only she could ask instead if Mr. Brice was looking for a bride and how he might feel about a dowry-less woman.

"Don't believe the rumors of him being a hermitic goblin. He's merely a busy man with few social interests. I'm conducting the initial reconnaissance, for he does not want a shallow or greedy wife. And yet, how does one disguise boundless wealth?"

"Yes, I see your point. It's a pity he doesn't join the party, though. The few older gentlemen in attendance are receiving all the attention." She laughed when he stared blankly back at her. "You see, the ladies believe any of the elderly men could be the viscount in disguise."

Mr. Brice's shoulders shook with laughter. "As if he were a grand prize. Age? Pox scars? Hunched back? Nothing dissuades a woman from a wealthy match. And yet, here you sit in the library with a solicitor. You're a curiosity, Lady Evelyn."

Blushing, she stared down at her folded hands. "My family put me up to accepting the invitation. They're desperate for me to make a good match, a wealthy match, as you aptly said. We've no money, you see. At least not much, not enough to sustain us for another year. And so, here I am. But I've not the heart for it, not when my interest is otherwise engaged."

With a long look to Mr. Brice, she gifted a tentative smile.

He returned it.

Two more days of secret meetings passed. Evelyn avoided the crowd following an aged guest, a man who hobbled on a cane and scowled, insisting he was not a viscount. The ladies were undeterred.

The day before the masquerade, she met her suitor in the north tower. Though he brought a canvas and paints, not a single stroke met the untouched surface.

Instead, Evelyn found herself backed against the stone wall, her fingers grasping Mr. Brice's hair as he molded his form to hers and sought her lips. His mouth slanted over hers in a warm embrace, his tongue teasing her lips open.

However difficult it would be to face her family, she could not marry for wealth. This was what she wanted. This feeling. This man.

The morning of the masquerade, he caught her before descending the stairs and pulled her into an empty parlor. Hugging her to him, his lips pressed to her temple, he asked what she would do if Viscount Marr chose her as his bride.

"Don't be silly, Stephen. He has no reason to choose me. I've avoided everyone and all entertainments."

"All the more reason to choose you. You're not swayed by greed or society. What will you do if he names you?" he persisted.

She pulled off his spectacles and looked into the depths of his eyes. "He won't choose me." As he made to speak again, she said, "If he does, I'll simply say no."

"In front of all invited, in front of your aunt, to the despair of your family, you would turn down a fortune and a title?" His brows furrowed, his tone incredulous. "For…for me? A no-name solicitor?"

"You're not a no-name solicitor. You're Stephen Brice, and I love you."

The evening of the masquerade brought all manner of fancy dress. Fey, vegetables, literary characters, and jesters mingled. Evelyn searched for the only person she wished to see. Her eyes fell on a figure in a domino, stooped, cane in hand. Stephen's worried questions echoed as the cloaked figure in black watched her, stalking her through the ballroom, never letting her out of his sight, his mask concealing his identity.

Anxiety churned her stomach. What if Stephen already knew what was to happen? What if the viscount chose her? It was one thing to tell herself she would refuse him, but it was quite another to do it.

Had she the courage to say no to a viscount? Much less in front of all these people. Her aunt's face could be her undoing, for in that face would be both disappointment and fear. Evelyn's entire family depended on her making the right choice.

Guests swirled on the dance floor, bold in their movements with their faces disguised. Not once did she see Stephen. The viscount, however, hovered on the fringes, watching. Whispers rose in crescendo as all realized he was in attendance.

Evelyn's pulse raced as the longcase clock struck midnight. The orchestra stilled. The tapping of a cane echoed. All eyes turned to watch the domino ascend the steps at the end of the ballroom.

In a creaking voice, the figure said, "It is time to choose my bride. May you all rejoice with me."

She was bumped and jostled as the crowd gathered before him. Aunt Augusta pushed to reach her niece, grabbing Evelyn's arm and patting her hand. In this moment, all their financial problems could be resolved.

This was the moment, her aunt repeated. This was the moment.

Evelyn's eyes fixed on the viscount. Her heart pounded. Her palms perspired in her worn gloves.

"Allow me to introduce the bride of my choice," his lordship said, deep voice crackling. "Would Lady Evelyn Woodward join me?"

Evelyn remained rooted. Gasps and mutterings enveloped her. Aunt Augusta squeezed her hand and pushed her forward, tears at the corners of her eyes. Before Evelyn knew what was happening, she was being propelled towards the viscount. A wave undulated through the crowd, thrusting her onward.

No, no, no. Why were her feet still moving? Why was she approaching him? No!

Her heart and her mind battled as her legs betrayed her. A glance behind her caught Aunt Augusta's hopeful expression. Her family depended on her. This was their chance.

She looked up at the cloaked man. A gloved hand reached out. Pausing before the steps, Evelyn stared at the hand, her own trembling and hesitant. What of Stephen? What of love?

But what of her family?

Her betrayal lanced through her.

Squeezing her eyes shut, she slipped her hand into the viscount's.

The grip was firmer than she expected as it tugged her up the stairs. She looked to the mask staring sightlessly at her.

"No," she whispered.

His head tilted to one side. "No?"

Afraid of her own words and the fate she was forging, she said with a tremor, "I will not marry you, your lordship."

"Is it my age?" he asked.

As silence stretched, she prayed Stephen's affection was sincere. "I'm in love with your solicitor."

While the crowd strained to hear the exchange, the viscount chuckled.

Straightening, he rose before her into a towering man. Releasing her hand, he removed his tricorn and mask and tossed them aside.

She gasped, the sound rippling through the crowd. Stephen stood before her, smiling, a cane in one hand, his other outstretched to take hers once more.

He bowed over her knuckles and said loud enough for all to hear, "Allow me to introduce myself. Stephen Brice, Viscount Marr."

"But…but…" Evelyn stuttered.

The room was abuzz.

"I apologize for my betrayal. I had to be sure you wanted me. I *am* a solicitor, you should know. I inherited this summer upon the death of my great uncle." Stephen winked. "Will you still marry me?"

With a jubilant cry, she threw her arms around his neck. For all the guests to see, Lady Evelyn kissed her true love.

Highwayman

My dearest Estella,

*Mourning ended yesterday. No longer must I feign
sorrow. Do not think your dearest friend wicked or
unchristian. For too long I sought the good in my
husband. For too long I hid the pain he caused me.
His death was a welcomed release, embraced with
tears of relief. Today, I shed the cloak of gloom. My
cousin arrives on the morrow to fetch me, for it
would seem a widow should not live alone. Hoping
to see you during the Season.*

Your Faithful Friend, Laura

Estella,

*I write to you from an inn between my old home
and my new one. Cousin arrived punctually.
The journey is tedious in his company. He is a
kind, staid gentleman. For all that, you will be
surprised when I say he proposed within the first*

hour. Yes, dearest Estella, the dullest gentleman of my acquaintance has proposed. My heart did flutter, but only from the resulting indigestion.

As politely as I might, kerchief in hand, did I dab at my eyes sorrowfully and say, "But my dear Lord Bluton has too soon passed from my heart. Give me time, Cousin." To which, he replied, "Lord Bluton would desire your security. Do reconsider my offer."

Only just have I been freed from my bonds, and now another wishes to capture me! I will not give in.

Your Determined Friend, Laura

My dearest friend,

Oh, Estella! Such monstrous adventure! I write to you from the safety of an inn near my family home. It shan't be long before I am safe in the bosom of my parents. But that is the last place I wish to be. What has happened to prompt this letter, you ask? A highwayman, Estella!

He came upon us after nightfall. A man in black. He seized the carriage, wrested the door from my cousin's grip, and with one hand pulled my cousin free of his seat. Grunts, shuffling feet, and hushed tones ensued. I knew not what I heard.

Quiet followed, a strangled quiet that had me biting my knuckle. I was afeared, Estella! Oh, how my heart did pound. What happened next, you ask? You shall think me mad or else a fibber.

A masked face thrust into the carriage. He must have been startled to see me, for he paused to take my measure. In that moment, I knew not fear — only yearning. It was his eyes, Estella. Eyes not of danger but of adventure and daring. Though I could not see his face to know if he were hideous or handsome, I fell for his eyes. I said to him with my own, "Take me with you!" Perchance he does not read eyes, for his response was a gentlemanly bow before departing.

Fear not for my staid cousin, for the dullard returned to the carriage before long, scuffed but unharmed. He mumbled about spies then told me not to worry my fair head when I queried his meaning.

I wonder if I shall see those eyes again. Oh, how I long for an adventure! Do you think me mad, Estella? I do not believe him a highwayman. Fanciful tales I have weaved since I saw him, but I do believe he is a spy for Crown and country! Though what he should want with my cousin, I know not.

Your Lovestruck Friend, Laura

Estella,

I am bored silly. The country assemblies are nothing more than rooms of dolts and boobies. I wish not for their company. Cousin has applied for my hand twice more. I want to escape. I want to live. I want to be free of these fools.

When Lord Bluton passed, I knew my chance had arrived. And yet, here I sit at the escritoire, wasting away of boredom. Return soon to regale me with tales from the continent. Certainly, you are having more fun than I. If I stole a horse and paced the King's road, do you suppose a highwayman with daring eyes would rescue me?

Your Bored Friend, Laura

My darling Estella,

This shall be my last letter for I know not how long. Do not fret for my safety – I am launching myself into an adventure!

Last night's assembly was another dull affair. The same dances, the same partners, the same jests. But then, a late arrival was announced, a Lord Rohr. At first, I did not turn, for what is one more dullard? Words flitted around me – rogue, beast, spy. It was the one word I longed to hear.

I turned, and what do you think I saw? The eyes. *Eyes of daring cut across the room to settle on me. Around the perimeter, he prowled, resolute. I knew, then, my adventure was about to begin. With steady, determined steps, he came upon me. With a bow and mocking smile, he said, "Come."*

And I did.

Enigmatic Earl

T*he Earl of Pennington*. She mouthed his name as her fingers clenched the edges of her pelisse.

Only one type of man arranged a marriage with a mousy spinster sight unseen — a desperate one. A *deranged* and desperate one. And that was exactly what the Earl of Pennington was rumored to be — deranged. Gazing out the carriage window, Aida shivered deeper into her coat. The frost-coated world stared back, as bleak as her future.

The carriage rocked to a stop. Startled from her reverie, Aida turned to the other window. Before her towered an Elizabethan manor, all diamond windows and symmetrical towers. With trembling hands, she tightened her hairpins and pinched her cheeks.

Bright light flooded the interior as a shadowed figure opened the door and offered to hand her down. *The earl?* she wondered, her breath catching. Blinking, a foot on the steps, a hand in his, she allowed her eyes to adjust.

Pursed lips and beady eyes observed her descent.

The man at her side said in way of a greeting, "If you'll follow me. His lordship is indisposed but requests you join him in the dining room at eight. I am Mr. Mueller, his lordship's secretary. Should you need aught, ring for me."

So, his lordship could not be bothered to meet his bride. Hardly an auspicious beginning.

Wordless, she nodded and followed, her maid in their wake.

One timbered hall after another, they walked until they came to an ornate door. With a bow, the man retired. Aida's first impression of the room was that life as a countess might not be bad after all. In fact, she could not immediately recall why she had hesitated to say yes when her father first apprised her of the situation. The hearth dominated one wall, the four-poster bed the other. What warmed the room was not the fire but the ceiling-to-floor tapestries, richly hued, each depicting a mythological scene. Her future brightened.

Only an hour did she remain in the chamber. Eight o'clock was eight hours away, after all. Feeling refreshed, although it had not been a lengthy drive from the inn at which she had stayed the night, she set out to explore her new home. Fingers laced at her waist, she ambled down the hall, peering out one casement window at a time. The next hall brought walls of mirrored portraits. Upon each she looked, admiring a ruff here and a banyan there.

When Aida turned the corner, she heard a voice, a low rumble of baritone. A door flanked by Doric columns hid the source. The rumble reverberated inside, echoing in crescendo.

Cold wood bit her ear as she pressed herself against the door.

"Your eyes sparkle of starlight, your teeth straight and unstained. I ask again, will you be mine?"

A high-pitched, nasal voice replied, "You, sir, are as dashing as a toad."

A third voice with a posh intonation said, "Clearly, old man, she's not moved by your perfumed words."

Behind the door clunked a chair, then footsteps, the shuffle of movement. Aida stumbled away from the door. Smoothing the length of her dress and touching a hand to her hair, she expected at any moment guests to queue and find the new mistress before them. When no one opened the door, she pressed ear to wood once more.

Silence.

A tender push was all that was needed to open the door and peer inside. A slight creak of the floorboard beneath her feet brought no one's attention. The room appeared empty at first glance. But no, not empty. The scratch of a quill perked her ear. Leaning in, she eyed the far corner.

A mop of hair in disarray was her only sight above a desk. Where were the guests? Sweeping her gaze around the room, she saw two doors into which they could have ventured.

Aida nearly leapt backwards at the *crack* of wood against wood. The gentleman's chair met an unwarranted fate against the wall as he pushed himself to stand, grumbling and muttering to himself. Aida shrank farther behind the protection of the door to remain unseen.

He prowled the room, pacing, circling, snarling.

Wisps of black strands shadowed a face already dark with stubble. Lengthy tresses frizzed a halo about his head. No coat or waistcoat adorned his torso, only a shirt, sleeves rolled to the elbow.

The earl.

She recognized him by reputation. Although she knew not his ailment, for it was not whispered on wagging tongues, she knew this must be her betrothed. As he paced, muttering to himself, mumblings punctuated only by curses, he fisted his hair and strangled the locks, leaving it more disheveled than before.

Oh dear. Oh no. There must be a way to escape. But to where? Could she reason with him for why she would make a terrible wife? This man could not possibly be her husband until death did them part. He was feral! To look this way before guests was unconscionable. And what of the bestial behavior? This would not do.

Pulling the door to a silent resolution, she fled the scene to the safety of her bedchamber.

Not until the longcase clock chimed eight did she venture out once more. Dressed her best, her heart in her throat, she followed a footman down the main stairs and to the dining room. All her fretting could not have prepared her for the man standing at the head of the table. Had she not halted her progress at the sight of him, she would have stumbled on her feet and made a cake of herself in the first meeting.

The man before her, greeting her with a bow, was immaculate. The wild tresses were combed back, held by a blue ribbon at the nape of his neck. He wore a form-fitting ensemble of matching blue. Aida was transfixed. His cheeks were smooth, his eyes smiling in welcome.

"My lady," he said. "Join me."

Two gulps and a mental shake.

How she took her seat or began the first course, she could not say. Her attention was fixed on him.

"You find your room satisfactory?" he asked between bites.

"Yes," she answered dumbly.

Although he waited for her to say more, she could not form the words. How was one to speak to such a handsomely perfect man after witnessing him in his madness? Was there some bit of trickery, perhaps a twin brother? She smiled to herself at such silliness.

"You find the meal amusing, Lady Aida?"

Oh no! A hand to her lips, she flushed. All this worry that he would ruin the meal, and it was she who was embarrassing herself.

When she did not reply, he asked, "Would the end of the week be agreeable to you for our wedding in the estate chapel? I thought it might give you time to accustom yourself to the estate, the staff, and —" he paused as though to recall the final words not yet spoken, "and to me."

"Yes, the end of the week." She stared at her plate, anxious.

If her betrothed were to be *this* man rather than the one she had seen in the study, how different would be her future, for never could she have imagined such an attractive man for herself. Now that he had met her and realized how ineffectual she was, how plain, he would surely change his mind and send her home. And how humiliating it would be to return. If only he knew how ferocious was her mind, full of ideas and opinions.

"Are there guests at the estate?" she asked rather than speak her mind.

At his arrested look, she bit her tongue, realizing she might have revealed her eavesdropping.

"Guests?" His brows furrowed in perplexity before rising in dawning. "Ah, you must mean Mr. Mueller's family. Yes, they're staying in the east wing until their cottage roof is repaired. You're fortunate to have missed the season's heavy snow."

Her polite smile, disguised with tight lips, settled them into a lengthy and uncomfortable silence. One million questions she wanted to ask, beginning with, *who's the madman in the third-floor study, for it cannot be you, can it?* But all she could do was rearrange her meal with gilded cutlery.

"No, that won't work," he mumbled under his breath during the final course.

Aida turned to her betrothed and was about to ask what would not work before he spoke again.

Shaking his head in frustration, he argued, "Yes, yes, it will."

Concerned, she watched him set down his cutlery and mutter incoherence, words she could neither hear nor understand. With a flourish of his napkin, he stood, his chair knocking backwards with a clatter.

"Yes, that's it. Yes, I have it." He took two steps from the table then about-faced. With a vacant expression, he said, "Excuse me."

Aida stared at his retreating back, stunned. He was deranged!

The next day brought Aida no sense of relief. However immaculate he had appeared at supper, there was no denying a beast lurked behind his eyes.

In her exploration of the house and garden, she avoided the hall with the study, not wanting to witness him in a madness, preferring the fiction of the evening without its strange conclusion. Remembering his staid visage at the table could almost convince her all was as it should be.

Not until supper did she see him again. He was as immaculate as the evening prior. She could not deny the thump of her heart at the sight of him. For four London Seasons she feared no one would have her, not dowdy Aida, whom no one gave a second glance or a second dance. For the two quiet years after, she knew her fate sealed. Now, could this man be hers?

"You must be wondering," he said between the first and second course, "why I arranged the betrothal through correspondence rather than finding a bride in London or by other means."

She squeaked a noncommittal answer.

"I'm a busy man. I've no time for socializing," he justified. "I also desire a wife who speaks her mind, a trait that comes with maturity, I find. With my list of criteria, Mr. Mueller searched until he found the best match. You."

His gaze lingered on her, although she could not say if he was admiring her "maturity" or suspecting he had chosen the wrong bride if he wanted a wife who would speak her mind. Aida wanted to speak with candor. Such ideas she had! And yet she remained mute, bashful under his scrutiny.

As with the evening prior, the two lapsed into silence until he chose to carry on a lively conversation with himself under his breath. So enraptured by his own mutterings, he seemed to forget her presence until, once again, he removed himself from the table with a hasty bow.

On the third day, Aida chose not to fear the earl's domain. If the beast was to be her husband in a few days' time, she could not fear him. Determined, chin raised, fingers clenched, she set off for the study. He could be elsewhere, of course. He could be anywhere but the study.

"'Tis the sparkle of starlight in your eyes and the perfume of your breath. I ask again, will you be my blushing bride?"

Aida stopped before the door, tugging her lower lip between her teeth. Was this not what she had heard days before?

Pressed to the door, she heard the same pinched tones.

"Nay, you knave! You've the manners of a toad."

The same third voice said, "Clearly, old man, she's not moved by your prosody."

The first gentleman responded with a laugh. "You doubt my sincerity, milady? When I come to you on bended knee and accept the abuse of you and brother both?"

A commotion ensued inside the room — shuffling of feet, a *thud*, the rifling of paper, a growl. Footsteps echoed across the room, approaching the door.

Approaching the door!

Aida leapt back and scurried down the hall in hopes the guests would not think her snooping. The door flung wide with a crack of wood against wall. Out stepped the beast.

Beneath the mane of wild hair, he entered the hall snarling and cursing. With long strides, he turned the corner away from her, never looking her direction. She pressed a hand to her breast and exhaled relief.

But then heavy footsteps returned, the string of curses preceding. When he turned back into the hall, he saw her standing with hand to bosom. Without missing a step, he growled and reentered the study, sealing the door behind him.

It took long moments to recover. From what, exactly, she could not say. Fear of discovery? Humiliation at snooping on guests? Confirmation that her betrothed was mad? Certainly being snarled at factored into the equation, for it was not every day she faced bared teeth. The peculiar part was she did not think he saw her, not really, at least not *her*. He mistook her for staff most likely.

"Give me one good reason why I should marry you?" Came that high-pitched voice again.

"I'll do better than that. I'll give you two. Your eyes are made of starlight and your hair of silk and — "

"I'll not listen to one more word from you, you knave! I'm in love with the blacksmith."

If Aida thought the commotion of before had been dramatic, it was nothing to now. A foul string of obscenities followed the woman's confession, along with a clattering of objects. Neither wanting to intrude nor get involved in whatever chaos the beast hosted in the study, she could nevertheless not stop herself from cracking open the door and peering inside.

Her temple to the door, she leaned into the room. Her first sight was of the earl pacing the room again. Clenched fists grappled his hair as he argued, in one breath disagreeing and in the next agreeing.

Leaning farther still, she looked for the guests but saw no one. The room was empty save the earl.

"You, sir, are a fortune hunter!" screeched the banshee.

Aida's hand flew to her mouth as she realized the words came from the earl, who, in that moment, turned to no one in the room to reply in a different voice.

"I'm not a fortune hunter. I'm a man in love. Your eyes glimmer like starlight. And — devil take these lines!" In a fury, he stomped to the desk, crumpled a bit of parchment, and tossed it into the hungry flames of the fire.

Good heavens.

She realized in an instant his malady, something far worse than madness.

With bold steps, she walked into the room.

Fury turned on her in force, bellowing rage. "Get out! You know the rules. Never intrude when — " His words suspended between them. Eyes wide, the earl ran both hands through his hair, calming the strays. "I do beg your pardon. I thought you were one of the staff. Is there something you need? Shall I ring for the butler?"

"You're a writer." Firm words met his questions.

A smirk hinted at the corners of his lips. "A playwright, though I lack inspiration. My publisher calls this latest play trite. It's a comedy — is it not supposed to be trite?"

"Your publisher's brave to say such words to an earl."

He barked a laugh. "Never. I use a *nom de plume*. He's no idea who's behind the name. Join me?" Upturning a chair next to his desk, he made quick work of tidying strewn papers.

"You maintain the narrative of being deranged to keep your writing a secret," Aida surmised, accepting the seat next to his.

Knit brows and a curious gaze studied her as he propped an ankle over a knee and steepled his fingers. "Deranged? They say I'm deranged?"

Oh dear. This was her reward for candor.

Cheeks warming, she wrung her hands in her lap, no longer confident. "If you'll pardon my saying, you do look frightful, and your behavior is often, shall we say, distracted."

In slow movements, he stood to catch his reflection in the mirror above the hearth. A low chuckle rumbled. Pulling free a tangled ribbon, he combed his hair with deft fingers and tied it with a tidy bow. After running a hand over his morning's stubble, he shrugged in apology.

"Do you find me less than savory?" he asked, returning to his chair.

"Quite the opposite," she said, pressing cold palms to heated cheeks. "Although, I'm not certain I can marry a man who writes such contrived dialogue."

"Contrived...can't marry...what is this abuse?" He leaned forward, gripping the arms of his chair.

"Eyes of starlight? A knave and a toad? Really, my lord. Shall we conceive better lines?"

He stared at her in wonder. His silence stretched for so long, she worried she had overstepped.

"I see you now," he said, leaning into the chair. "Why are you hiding in drab clothes and behind a demure mask?"

"I beg your pardon?"

"I've been searching for you all my life. And yet, so wrapped up in my own obsessions, I didn't recognize you when you finally came to me. But I see you now." Pushing himself to his feet, he bowed with reverence. "You're my muse, Lady Aida. Now, inspire me."

Grabbing his quill, he readied a fresh page.

With fluttering heart, Aida shared her thoughts, feeling more alive with each of his smiles than she had in all her five and twenty years. For the first time, she was not a wallflower. He saw her. He knew her. And no longer was he the beast of rumor.

When the final candle guttered into the night, he leaned a rough cheek to hers and whispered, "How beautiful and brilliant you are when you speak your mind. Will you marry me as I am?"

"Those words, Andrew, are not contrived nor trite. I believe you've found your inspiration. Yes, I'll marry you."

Their eyes shone with the passion and intelligence of shared vision. Together, they would write the story of their life. His hair would never again be frizzed by his fingers, rather hers. They would live life through the scratch of a quill—between romps on the study floor, of course.

The Governess

Rain clattered against the windowpane, a rat-a-tat-tat accompanied by the drum of thunder and the chorus of wind. However dark was the sky, it was not yet dusk.

"I'm bored," said a young lady at the card table.

Frances did not look up from her sewing. The threaded needle moved in steady determination, repairing the hem of her charge's dress. The offending tear was the result of a valiant vault over the parlor table, performed with the skill that no gently born child of three ought to demonstrate.

"When is Miss Milli to arrive?" asked the same voice.

This time, Frances' eyes flitted to her employer. Mr. Rawleigh's expression remained unaffected, his attention on the hearth.

Today marked Mr. Rawleigh's thirty-third day of being, an occasion celebrated by a supper party. The guests had arrived early that afternoon before the storm struck, an equal number of young ladies to gentlemen except the missing Miss Milli, Mr. Rawleigh's intended. Although that was not entirely true. The two had yet to make an alliance, but it was on the tongues and in the glances of the guests — any moment he would propose, if only she would arrive.

Wealth married wealth, of course. It was all the two had in common, from Frances' estimation, though what did she know? She was only the governess. Her charges, two girls, were from Mr. Rawleigh's previous marriage, a love match as far as Frances had heard from the servants, a love match that left him bereft for the two years following her death. Perhaps Miss Milli could renew his spirits.

Frances swallowed, ignoring the pain in her heart to think of him married to Miss Milli, a silly girl indeed. But then, her heart ached at the thought of him married to anyone. Foolish sentiments. Frances was but a servant.

A gentleman stood and joined the two ladies at the card table. "She won't come now. The weather is atrocious. If she has any sense, she'll have stopped at the inn to wait out the storm."

A lady standing near the window scoffed. "Miss Milli? At an *inn*?"

A howl of wind rattled the windows until a footman closed the curtains. The room plunged into momentary darkness, another footman rushing to light the candles.

"You should go in search of her, Mr. Rawleigh, to see her to safety," another gentleman said.

In answer to the suggestion, a clap of thunder shook the walls. The ladies shrieked. The gentlemen flinched. Frances stabbed her finger with the needle.

Wincing, she searched her petticoat pocket for her handkerchief, only to recall she had given it to one of her charges before being summoned to the party. A drop of blood stared up at her from the tip of her finger. At least it did not hurt.

A pair of periwinkle shoes came into view in backdrop of her injured digit.

"Take mine," said a deep voice.

How had he known? She looked up to meet the eyes of her employer. Dark, penetrating eyes stared back. Without looking away, she took his proffered handkerchief and wrapped it about her finger.

With a nod, Mr. Rawleigh turned his back to her. "I propose a game of pantomimes to occupy our minds from the storm."

"But we can't play without Miss Milli!" protested the ladies at the card table, seconded by at least two of the gentlemen.

"She could be delayed for the evening if the storm does not abate." Mr. Rawleigh clapped his hands and waved for the footmen to move furniture. "Let us make the most of our time. It is, after all, my birthday, and I wish for pantomimes."

Setting aside her work, Frances inched to the edge of her chair.

As the guests gathered around the makeshift stage, a pummeling knock echoed down the hall outside. All eyes turned to the parlor door. A commotion could be heard, voices raised, feet stomping on aged wood. Frances turned to Mr. Rawleigh. Startled, she realized he was looking back at her, a hesitation about his person, as though uncertain if he should go to the parlor door or come to her. But why would he come to her? She knew nothing of the cacophony beyond the room.

The parlor door opened, then, a hush descending on the room in stark contrast to the hubbub in the hall.

The butler, shoulders stooped with age, a gnarled hand resting on the door handle, cleared his throat. "There is a disturbance, sir."

Mr. Rawleigh's gaze moved between the butler to Frances and back before he bowed to all in the room and followed the butler.

The parlor erupted in volcanic voices, each word hot with anger and curiosity — who dared disturb them on such an evening? Who dared barge into the manor uninvited? Who dared call on Mr. Rawleigh while he was entertaining?

In the silence of her station, Frances slipped out of the parlor door to follow the noise in the hall, tucking the handkerchief into her pocket as she proceeded.

The noise rose in crescendo as she drew closer to the foyer. Mr. Rawleigh raised both hands to capture the attention of the crowd, and a crowd it was indeed. Bedraggled villagers, wet and disheveled, huddled together, voices ascending in distress.

"You can't turn us away," cried a woman. "The valley is flooding. We've nowhere to go."

A man with the shoulders of a farmer said, "The manor is the highest point."

Voices overlapped as Mr. Rawleigh continued to gain their attention. "Please, everyone, I've no intention of sending anyone away. You're safe from the storm. My staff will see to your comfort while I converse with Mr. Overhill about the extent of the flooding."

"They can't stay here!" screeched a shrill voice behind them.

Frances turned to see the partygoers crowded in the hallway and looking at the villagers in dismay.

"They're dripping on the floor, sir. Remove them at once," ordered one of the guests, wrinkling her nose.

Knowing Mr. Rawleigh as she did, which was to say not well, although he was as devoted a father as anyone could ask for, she could not say what compelled her to join the conversation. The sight of the villagers? The fear of the storm? The anger of the guests? The humbleness of her station?

Frances turned to her employer, distraught and wringing her hands. "You simply can't send them away. Allow me to see to their needs." When a raised eyebrow was her response, she added a whispered, "Please."

Mr. Rawleigh nodded to the butler. Stooped though the butler was, he orchestrated a variation on the theme of hospitality *afectuosamente*. Without missing a beat, Frances offered her arm to an older woman, leading her and her family to the kitchen so everyone could warm themselves by the fire until arrangements could be made.

Before the troupe made it to the end of the hallway, another knock interrupted the party. The guests, who were up in arms about the villagers being sheltered under the same roof, began another loud protest at the continuous interruption of their frivolity. Mr. Rawleigh himself wrenched open the door.

The voice that greeted him was panicked, each word sputtered between huffs of breath, the man clearly winded. "Miss Milli, sir. The carriage overturned in the storm. She and her mother are trapped inside."

Without a backward glance to guests or villagers, Mr. Rawleigh stepped into the downpour, the front door slamming behind him.

It was more than half an hour before Mr. Rawleigh returned. Frances had seen to the comfort of the villagers and listened to more than her fair share of tales of flooding in the valley, homes gutted with water, livestock lost, brave sons seeing beast and burden to safety amidst the chaos. Considering all that had occurred, a strange stillness had settled in the house. Even the guests in the parlor were eerily quiet.

Frances watched the door in anticipation, each moment stretching longer than the last. She worried more for Mr. Rawleigh's safety than the young girl, which was unchristian of her, but a truth she could not deny. The storm, if possible, had worsened since his departure. Even from the ground floor, she could hear the rain pelting the roof and feel a disconcerting vibrato with every gust of wind and rumble of thunder.

With a slap of wood against wood, the front door flung open. Sheets of rain blanketed the foyer. Miss Milli cradled in his arms, Mr. Rawleigh stormed into the manor, black hair matted to his face, his clothes soaked through.

A moment of uncertainty delayed Frances. The sight of him pounded her heart; the sight of him carrying the young lady stilled her limbs; the sight of the limpness with which Miss Milli lay chilled her bones. The girl was as pale as the dress she wore, her eyes closed, her lips slightly parted.

"Follow me," Frances said, collecting herself.

They went to the second floor, where the guest rooms had been readied. Vaguely, Frances could hear voices from the stairwell, the sounds of Miss Milli's mother and the household staff, Frances suspected. After a tug to the bellpull, Frances positioned herself next to the bed, watching with an aching heart as Mr. Rawleigh laid the girl on the bed with all the tenderness he could afford.

"We must get her warm," Frances said, and began rubbing Miss Milli's arms and hands.

Mr. Rawleigh watched in silence for half a minute before Frances nodded to Miss Milli's other arm. He hesitated, then reached to mimic Frances' movements. Not long did they work before two maids arrived, ready to do all that was necessary to help the girl.

Although her presence was unnecessary, Frances remained to help the maids even after Mr. Rawleigh departed to change and see to his guests. Even had the young lady not been her employer's presumed intended, she would have stayed. It was the right thing to do.

She was, however, surprised that she was the only one who remained in the room, aside from one of the maids. The mother never came to visit, likely already changed and in the parlor to work her wiles on Mr. Rawleigh. The other guests never came either. However ridiculous it was for Frances to pity a young lady who had everything, but pity her she did, for the girl's life seemed all fluff and no substance.

The only person who appeared to care was Mr. Rawleigh. Thrice over the next hour, he came, asking if Frances needed aught. It was her imagination that he seemed to be checking on *her* rather than on Miss Milli. Of course, he was checking on Miss Milli. What was a governess to him?

After two hours of Frances' vigil, Miss Milli's eyes fluttered opened, her cheeks warming with a pink tinge. The young lady groaned and turned her head.

In a groggy voice, she asked, "Who are you?"

Frances clasped Miss Milli's hand in her own. "Miss Frances Witherstone, governess. It is so good to see you awake. You gave us a fright."

Tugging her hand from Frances' grasp, Miss Milli frowned. "Governess? Why are you here?" The disdain in her tone needled Frances, not unlike the finger prick from earlier. "Where's Mama? Where's Mr. Rawleigh?"

With a curt nod, Frances removed herself from the bedside to fetch Mr. Rawleigh. She found him, as expected, in the parlor with the other guests, all with long faces—except Miss Milli's mother. The woman chirped into his ear as though her daughter were not upstairs rendered unconscious for hours.

He was the first to see Frances at the door. His eyes widened. His torso lifted.

Frances smiled.

All in the room took note of her in that moment and rushed past, nearly knocking her aside in their rush to quit the parlor and be the first to reach Miss Milli's sickbed. All except Mr. Rawleigh. His hands captured her upper arms as she stumbled backwards to avoid the stampede. Once he steadied her, he did not let go.

Frances looked into the eyes of her employer, her heartbeat erratic. They were alone. So close he stood, she could smell his shaving soap.

"You should go to her, sir," Frances said. "She's expecting you."

He shook his head. "It's for you I wait."

Frances furrowed her brows.

"You, Miss Frances Witherstone, are the strongest and most compassionate woman of my acquaintance.

I've long admired you, but not until today have I realized I've been mistaken in not voicing that admiration. Tell me now — do you wish for me to stand aside or speak my heart's desire?"

The worry wrinkling his brow melted any hesitation she should feel in confessing her feelings.

"I care for you, too," she admitted, her voice timid.

What would come next, she knew, would be a proposal to serve as mistress. How could she say no when she loved him beyond reason and had done so for over a year? Although her life would be lived as the ruined woman of his evenings, she could not say no. He may think her strong, but she was weak in resolve.

"Do you, Frances? Do you truly?" His eyes searched hers. "I suspected but couldn't be certain. I dared not speak for fear of losing you. It's not an easy position, ours." The rain provided a symphonic backdrop to his words. "Say you'll marry me, and I'll secure a license at the first sign of the sun."

"Marry you?" Frances took a step away, shaking her head in confusion. "*Marry* you? Have you gone mad? I'm a governess!"

He stepped forward, not allowing her to escape. A smile teased the corners of his lips. "It's the only way I'll have you. My lawfully wedded wife, the mother of my children, the mistress of my heart. Please, say you'll have me, society be dashed."

There was only one way to respond. She threw her arms about his neck. "I'm yours."

The Gypsy

T he betrothal dinner was a disaster. Not only was it pouring rain, but the bridegroom had not bothered to attend.

Felicia eyed each of the gentlemen in the drawing room—quizzing glasses, pomade, long noses, and starched shirt points. Any of them could be him. None had yet admitted to the honor. Her parents had arranged the marriage, thirsty for an alliance with a titled family, regardless of Felicia's wishes.

Today, at the dinner, she would meet her betrothed for the first time.

Or at least that was the plan. Except the inconvenient detail of him not having arrived.

Lightning flashed, sending one of the ladies into a fit of vapors. Felicia rolled her eyes. What she wanted was William by her side. He would share her humor, roll his eyes alongside her, poke fun at each of the stuffy gentlemen in attendance. Oh, William.

A fierce banging at the front door stole everyone's attention. Howling wind played accompaniment, the percussion of thunder completing the symphony.

Bang. Bang. Bang. The knocker sounded in earnest.

A chill tickled down Felicia's spine. Her betrothed?

Outside of the drawing room came a commotion of raised voices above the storm. With a nod to the startled guests, she headed for the hall. A mixture of relief, disappointment, and curiosity swept through her at the sad sight of the man standing at the front door. Had she expected it to be William, come to save her? Of course not. Standing in the entrance and arguing in a high-pitched wail was a gypsy with long, wet hair matted to his face. Hunched with a hump and favoring his left leg by leaning on the sorriest wooden cane Felicia had ever seen, he begged to be let inside.

He said to the butler, "The bridge has washed out, good sir. I'm stranded. I need shelter until the storm passes."

The guests crowded behind her, sniveling and snorting. What a sodden sight of horse dung, they whispered. Send him back into the rain, they argued.

The butler gave his best argument, trying to shut the door on the gypsy.

The stranger was not deterred. "Please, I can pay for the stay by telling the fortunes of these honored guests. A fortune for each, and then I'll be on my way."

Another argument ensued, but Felicia was intrigued. The chill tickled again. A warning or a nudge, she could not guess. Her fortune, did the man offer? Yes, her fortune indeed. She knew what her future held—a loveless marriage to some titled rogue. Still, there was something endearing about the fellow. Probably the cane.

"Let him stay," she instructed the butler. "See he's given dry clothes, and then show him to the parlor."

The butler gaped at her for but a moment, hesitating only long enough to show his disapproval. Her parents would be displeased, but she did not care. If they were to host a betrothal dinner for an arranged marriage, then the least she could do was have a little fun. Best get the gypsy into the parlor and settled telling fortunes before they heard the news.

With the guests returned to the drawing room, their excitement increased, each wanting to go in first to hear their fortune, never mind their misgivings minutes ago. Not long did they wait before the butler arrived to announce the gypsy was ready for the first guest, requesting the lady in yellow to come first. Felicia wore blue. The lady in yellow squealed, the envy of her peers, and disappeared through the connecting doors.

Ten minutes they waited. When the lady in yellow returned, she wore a sly smile.

"I'll be married in a month to a gentleman with the initial of R." She fluttered her eyelashes to both Lord Reynolds and Mr. Rinnard.

Next, one of the gentlemen swept through the doors. After another ten minutes, he returned, grumbling about a broken engagement in his future. Four more people had a turn before the butler called for Felicia.

The parlor was poorly lit, the curtains drawn, only two candle holders torched. The gypsy sat at a low table, hair still matted over his face. It looked as though they had fashioned him with bed linen rather than clothes, though anything must be superior to wet attire. The cane was propped against the chair, the hunch more prominent while seated. Poor, bedraggled soul.

"Join me," came a scratching voice.

Felicia sat across from him, taking in the shadows that hid his face. As he mumbled to himself, speaking to spirits beyond this realm, she thought she ought to feel fear. Instead, she sensed familiarity, as though she and the gypsy had shared moments before. Was this the workings of gypsy magic? Had he bewitched her to misinterpret the warning of her senses?

"There's a wedding in your future." His tone implied a grand revelation, a smugness to predicting her future.

"You'll have to do better than that." Felicia smirked. "Anyone could have told you this is a betrothal party, *my* betrothal."

Nodding, the shadow said, "But not anyone would have told me your heart belongs to another."

Felicia stiffened. No one could know that. *No one.*

"I see by your reaction, I'm correct." A low cackle grated the air. "Would it surprise you that the same would be true for all of your guests? Too easy, Lady Felicia. Ah, but I've shocked you again, for I know your name. Could I not have heard it from a guest? How easily you are all fooled."

"I think it best you leave now." Felicia made to stand, but a hand shot across the table and grabbed her wrist.

"Here's something I can offer that's not a trick. For a kiss, I can take you to the one you love."

What a charlatan!

Outraged and huffing, Felicia freed her hand and stood. "Your company is no longer welcome."

In a deep voice, no longer raspy or pinched, but a velvet bass that caressed her heart, he asked, "Is your betrothed not welcome then?"

Felicia gasped when the man rose from his chair, flinging off the linen and pillowed hunch. Hidden beneath was an impressively tailored suit. He swept the hair from his face and grinned.

"William!"

She flung herself into his waiting arms. What a scoundrel to have tricked her!

"Oh, William! It's been so long. Hold me." The arms about her tightened. "What will we do? I'm engaged. It's all arranged, the paperwork signed."

"Yes, I know, for you're engaged to me."

Leaning away from him, she stared, incredulous. "Whatever do you mean? My parents would never agree to that."

"Did I never mention my eccentric great-uncle? It would seem he died without an heir. Before you stands the newest made viscount, a convenient title I used to seduce your parents into agreeing to the contract, sight unseen. They've no idea they've betrothed you to the very man they sought to ruin. Is this a good surprise?"

She cupped his face in her hands. "You know it is! But you're naughty for not telling me."

"I'll show you naughty yet. Now, where's my kiss?"

The Gift

Baron Overland paced at the window overlooking the apple orchard. For the past fifteen minutes, he had listened to their approach, pots banging, bugles trumpeting, voices raised in song. His first fear had been they would come to the door. He instructed his butler to send them off with a flea in their ear should they bring their merriment here. They did not. Instead, they made for the orchard.

With an anxious glance over his shoulder, he eyed his son. Nine-year-old Gabriel sat on the floor of the upstairs drawing room, doodling an artistic masterpiece with a bit of chalk.

Owen turned back to the window, holding aside the damask curtain to peek outside. The villagers gathered around one of the largest apple trees and sang of the harvest, angering the baron with each note. How dared they trespass? Since moving into the estate six months prior, he had not set foot in the village and had turned away all callers. Could they not see he did not want their company?

Cursed merrymakers! They had no right to be on his land, making an unholy din.

As the noise reached a crescendo, his fingers curled into fists. So help him, if they dared upset —

Chalk flew across the room, narrowly missing Owen's head. His son screeched and wailed, hands cupping his ears. Feet kicked at the floor as the boy tried to silence the commotion. Rushing across the room, Owen grasped his son's upper arms to pull him into a cradled hug.

"Gabe, all is safe," he said above the noise outside and the shrieks inside. "Settle against my chest."

He drew his boy to him, but Gabriel had other plans. The boy kicked at his father, landing a hearty blow to the gut, his cries rising.

That did it. No more trespassers.

"I'll stop the noise."

The baron nodded to the nurse in the corner to look after his son while he dealt with the villagers. The nurse was his least favorite person. She was afraid of the boy, but she had been the only one to accept the position. Owen devoted his days to looking after Gabriel himself. The nurse was merely a helper, someone for moments like this when Owen had no choice but to leave his son unsupervised.

Growling, Lord Overland stormed out of the drawing room, down the stairs, and out the front door. Snow crunched beneath his boots. Wind bit at his exposed cheeks. Anger fueled his veins, armoring him against the cold.

As he drew nearer to the group, he waved his arms over his head and shouted. It took long moments to be heard over their song. When their faces turned, his ire rose. Nosy, busybody, do-gooding villagers. They had no right to force their merriment. Did the manor display greenery? Had he invited them? He cursed under his breath as he drew closer.

"Get off my land! You're trespassing!" he shouted. "Take your merrymaking elsewhere. Go away!"

Additional threats flew through his mind—*I'll release the hounds. I'll have stable hands chase you with pitchforks.* He settled for a steely glare intended to frighten them away.

Muffled protests rippled through the crowd. A few turned away without argument. The one brave soul who stepped forward sent Owen's eyebrows high on his forehead.

A little girl of perhaps five or six years of age pushed through the villagers and said, with her chin held high, "We're woswing. For the holevest."

Schooling his features for a menacing glare, he said, "No wassailing on my property. Take your harvest well wishes somewhere else."

A young woman with flaxen hair and kind eyes joined the girl. In another lifetime, he would have thought her pretty. More than pretty, in fact. She was startlingly lovely, as though the angels on high smiled on her, leaving a radiant glow about her windpinkened cheeks. Owen shook the nonsense from his head and glowered at her.

She tilted her head and said, "We apologize for disturbing you, my lord. We only thought to wish you well." With that, she ushered the little girl away, nodding to the villagers around her to leave without further protest.

Victorious, the baron returned to the house and took two steps at a time back to the drawing room. His first sight was of the nurse, facing the door with hands clasped. The second sight was of the otherwise vacant room. His heart skipped a beat.

"Where's Gabe?"

"I'm so sorry, my lord, I—"

"Where. Is. Gabe." His words were sharp, controlled, but inside he panicked.

"He followed you. From the window, I saw him heading for the orchard. I was sure he found—"

Owen did not hear the remainder of her words. Darting back downstairs, he flung open the front door.

He slammed full body into someone. When he steadied himself and the other person, he realized it was the young lady with the flaxen hair. Two wide-eyed children stood behind her, along with a couple of other villagers.

Frantic, he said, "My son. I need to find my son."

Steady on their feet, he released his hold of the woman and raced past, his destination the orchard. He called his son's name. Although he tried to listen for a reply, all he could hear was fear roaring in his ears. He ran. He called. He searched. Nothing.

Then, from somewhere behind him, he heard someone else shouting his son's name. The woman. Then the children. Then the villagers. More voices joined. A choir of his son's name.

Hot tears stung his eyes as he ran from tree to tree, calling for Gabriel.

Snow began to fall. His son would be cold without a coat, his feet blue without boots. He would be frightened. He would be alone.

"We found him! My lord, here!"

Owen spun in circles, searching for the voice. Then from the far end of the orchard trekked a group of the wassailers, torches held high, arms waving. Gabriel led them, his hand held by the flaxen-haired woman. In seconds, Owen reached them, scooping his son into his arms and resting the boy's head on his shoulders. Gabe, for all his father's trouble, giggled.

The baron wanted to thank the villagers. He wanted to embrace the woman. He wanted… He wanted his son safe and warm and away from ridicule.

"Excuse me," he said to the group and fled back to the manor.

The next morning, Owen sat with Gabriel, both enjoying cups of chocolate, wisps of steam curling about their noses and sending Gabe into fits of laughter. The baron's heart swelled to see his son smile.

Not since before his wife's death two years ago had Gabe been happy. Explaining why she would not return had been more difficult than raising the child on his own. No one had tried to make her passing easy for Lord Overland or his son, not his peers, not his neighbors, not his younger brother or nephews, and most pointedly not his wife's parents, Gabriel's grandparents. *Institutionalize* was the word on their lips, their eyes narrowed at the then seven-year-old.

And so, he left them all behind, making a new home here. If they kept to themselves, no one could judge them or utter again that dreaded word Owen would never consider.

"I want to play," Gabe said over his cup of chocolate, a hand raised to rub his forehead.

His words for anyone else might have sounded jumbled, a little slurred even, but to Owen, he heard only the clarity of Gabriel's desire for love and friendship, something only Owen could give, not other children, not villagers, only Owen.

The drawing room door opened.

"Callers at the door, my lord," said the butler.

Owen scowled. "And you've not gotten rid of them?"

"They're here for Master Gabriel, my lord."

"They're...*what*?" Setting his cup on the table, he looked from his son back to the butler.

"Callers for Master Gabriel," repeated the infuriating man before he bowed out of the room.

Looking back to his son, he made to give an excuse why he must leave the room for a moment, but Gabe had understood to some degree what the butler said. The boy set his cup on the table with such force the chocolate sloshed over the edges. He squealed and ran for the door before Owen could stop him.

"For me! For me!" Gabe cried, running down the stairs for the front door.

Owen pursued.

Both he and his son stopped at the bottom of the stairs. Standing in the entrance hall was the woman, the two children, an older couple, and a puppy.

Gabe turned to hide his face against Owen's waistcoat.

The young woman with her kind eyes and angel-touched visage stepped forward with a curtsy. "As there's no one to introduce us, I hope you'll pardon the informality. I'm Miss Hannah Flowers." Gesturing to the older couple, she said, "Mr. and Mrs. Moon. And these two are my nephew and niece, Mr. Murphey and Miss Myrtle. We've come with a gift for Gabriel." She patted the little girl on the back.

Miss Myrtle held up her arms, the puppy's back feet peddling the air, its tail wagging. "This is Wodwick."

She set young Roderick on the floor so he could snuffle his way to Gabriel, the latter who peeked past his father's waistcoat to see the droopy eyed dog.

"Please?" begged Gabriel, his almond-shaped eyes blinking.

"Go on then," Owen said.

His son hopped down the last few steps then dropped to the floor to greet Roderick. The other two children did not wait for permission but launched themselves across the entrance hall at Gabriel to ask him to play with them and be their friend.

Owen could do little more than stare. Manners forgotten, guests ignored, he watched his son. The children accepted him without question, without judgement, without fear. The trio carried on as children did, taking turns rubbing the puppy's stomach and exclaiming about making snowmen.

Miss Hannah Flowers took four more steps forward. "We hope it's not cheeky of us to bring such a gift. You're not afraid of dogs, are you?"

For the first time in years, Owen's lips twitched into a smile. "No. I'm not afraid of dogs."

"Splendid. That's a relief." She turned to Mr. and Mrs. Moon with a smile, a smile that flipped Owen's stomach upside down. Turning that smile on him, she said, "We're so pleased finally to meet you, Lord Overland. You've been quite the mystery for us."

"Papa!" Gabe said, laughing and tugging at Owen's hand. "Snowmen!"

The baron raised his brows to his guests. They all looked from each other to the children and nodded.

"Not without your coat," he said to his son who had already begun to whoop with delight.

The children, puppy in tow, led the adults outside to play in the snow.

Mr. and Mrs. Moon stood next to the baron, watching his son with glistening eyes. Mrs. Moon said, "He's like our grandson, my lord. A blessing in the disguise of a child. A gift."

With a sharp turn of his head, Owen asked, "Like my son? You mean—"

"He's not so alone in the world, my lord, although until last night we'd never seen anyone like our grandson. It makes our heart happy. Our daughter living up north, we rarely see him. He's a good boy. Always happy. Always full of love."

Owen did not know what to think. Here stood three individuals who accepted his son without judgement, who looked on the boy as a blessing rather than a curse, who brought gifts rather than physicians.

The children did not shrink from Gabe as had his own flesh and blood. Instead, they stacked snow together as though Gabe were one of them, as though he were a friend they had known for years, the puppy yipping at their ankles as stubby legs sank into the snow.

Miss Hannah Flowers packed snow in her hand. "Do you think you could be happy in our little village?"

He studied her, wondering what life would be like with friends for Gabe, friends for himself, a young woman in need of courting. "Yes, I believe I can and will be happy here. Because of you, Miss Flowers, I have reason to hope."

Their gazes locked and lingered, a deepening rose rouging her cheeks.

Then a snowball hit his chest.

Gabe shrieked, "Got you!"

To his shock, Miss Flowers grinned, pulled back her arm, and slung at her nephew the packed snow she had been handling. She ducked and dodged as her nephew sent two snowballs chasing her in vengeance.

Lord Overland laughed, the sound ringing in the snowy wonderland. A bright future shone before him, one with friendship, acceptance, and possibly even love.

The Apothecary

A witch, they called her.

Rupert did not believe in witches.

"Madame Esmerelda," creaked the sign above the cottage door, swaying in the breezeless air.

Hand on the handle, he shivered, an inexplicable chill tickling from nape to base.

For over a month, he had ignored the urge to come, pushing it deep inside. Each time he walked past the path leading to the cottage, he had averted his eyes, not willing to give into temptation, even going so far as to post an advertisement for a governess. Each day that the position remained unfilled, he lingered longer at the end of the path.

There was no such thing as a witch.

He pressed the handle.

The door opened with an inhale, breathing in the outside air with such force, Rupert was tugged inside. No sooner did both boots meet the cobbled floor than the door sealed behind him with an exhale. He blinked to adjust his sight. The smoke of tallow candles wreathed his head, the smell dizzying his senses. He licked parched lips.

"Come closer," said the intoxicating vapor.

As his eyes adjusted, he spied more shadows than objects. The room was spacious, the perimeter lined with jars, candles, and vials. From the smoky haze of the rafters, herbs and flowers hung.

"I know what you seek," the same voice said, a sultry tease had it not been for the overtones of a scratching nail across stone. "You want love."

Rupert squinted into the shadows, searching for the source of the voice.

Darkness persisted. "I have what you want." The words circled him, enticed him, trailing up his coat sleeve and whispering into his ear. "I am what you want."

A tickle at his neck.

He jerked away from the sensation, turning to face the apothecary. No magic, this. Before him stood a flesh and blood woman. Transfixed, he could not look away. The perfect woman—raven-haired, dark and mysterious, with curves he had no business admiring. She disarmed him with a glance of emerald green eyes, luminous and reflective, predatory and feline.

Tearing his eyes away, he studied a dusty jar on the sideboard. "No. I mean, yes, I seek a love potion, but not this. I seek a mother for my daughter, a companion for myself."

"You need a woman who will please you." With a sway of her hips, the Circe embodiment moved closer. "Someone to obey you. Someone to pleasure you."

"No." He aimed to sound firm, but his tongue was heavy and slow.

She moved closer yet, reaching a hand to him, palm open. "Beauty, sensuality, *love*. I have the perfect potion for you."

Forcing himself to focus against the swirling spells enchanting him, he said, "I'm not looking for love or beauty or…" He swallowed. "Sex." Meeting Madame Esmerelda's gaze, he continued, "No one can replace my late wife. I want someone for my daughter, someone to be a good mother for her. I want someone with whom I can find comfort."

He stopped before mentioning other characteristics. Intelligent, gentle, moral, he might have added. A soul as lost and lonely as he. But he said no more of the woman he sought, for the words he had spoken brought him to his senses. He should not have come.

Wordless, he turned to leave, his hand grasping the door handle.

Her voice receding farther into the room, she said, "The perfect potion for the perfect companion."

A clink of glass in the distance.

Before he could turn, a slender hand wrapped around his waist. Fingers unfurled to present a vial nestled in the open palm. He hesitated.

"On the next full moon, drink this. For the three nights following, chant:
'Helios, Hecate, and Circe,
Hear my cry.
Bring true love, not a lie.
Aphrodite, Ishtar, and Isis,
A companion I do seek.
A worthy mother, no one meek.
Hear my thoughts addressed to thee,
As my will so mote it be.'"

How the vial came to sit upon his bedside table, he could not recall, but he stared at it every night for a week, ignoring it with each snuff of his candle.

What silliness. That he had gone to the apothecary in the first place rankled him. That he had accepted the vial of whatever was in it — likely more goat urine than love potion — angered him. He did not believe in witches or spells or magic. Love potion indeed. What he needed was a devoted governess to raise his daughter, nothing more.

Or so he told himself for two more weeks.

The advertisement remained unanswered. His heart ached. His daughter moped. The full moon hung heavy in the sky, luminous and reflective.

If it was silliness, then what harm could come from it? That night, with a sneer and mocking arch of his brow, he downed the vial's contents, lavender flavored water from the taste. The three nights following, he chanted the lines. When his companion did not appear on the fourth day, he tossed the empty vial into the fire.

Days turned to a week, then another.

On the morning of the new moon, the front knocker struck the oak door. Rupert remained in the drawing room. Near the hearth, his daughter sketched, raising her art every so often for him to appraise.

The butler stepped into the drawing room with a bow. "A young woman to see you, sir. A candidate for governess."

Samantha squealed and clapped her hands. "A governess, Papa! For *me*!"

"Not yet, my sweet. Let me be the judge."

Rupert rose from his chair and signaled the butler to direct the guest to his study. This was the answer to his prayers, he told himself on the way to the study. A governess. Not a companion or a mother for Samantha. Not a creature of beauty and guiles fabricated from a love brew and chant. A sensible governess. He ignored the tickle that ran from the nape of his neck to the base of his spine, the secret desire that the woman who stepped over the threshold would be *perfect*.

Seated, breath held, he waited.

The young woman who stepped into the room shocked him to the core. He leaned forward, one hand on the arm of his chair, the other braced against the desk.

She was *scarred*.

A curtsy and a half smile greeted him. "Sasha, sir. My name's Sasha."

Manners. He tried to remember his manners. He stood, bowed, waved her to sit, then took his own seat, his eyes never wavering.

Early twenties, he would wager, but it was difficult to tell past the scarring that slashed across an oval face. One blue eye studied him, the other hazy, grey, and blind. From chin to forehead, puckered lines marred the skin, her lips limp at one corner, her hairline uneven with a bald patch where the marks licked at matted brown hair. He could not look away. Impolite of him, he knew, but he felt so great an internal rage at the injustices in the world to have robbed someone so young of a chance at a full life that he could not avert his eyes.

Entranced, he hired her before she finished reciting a well-rehearsed rationale for why she would make the perfect governess for the young mistress of the manor. There was little doubt in his mind Miss Sasha worried she would not be granted the position. She had neither experience nor references to recommend her. What she did have was an impressive history of academic studies, far beyond what Rupert would have expected.

Promptly, he escorted the new hire into the drawing room, eager to make introductions and hoping he had taught his daughter tact. From his peripheral, he saw Miss Sasha tuck the unscarred corner of her bottom lip between her teeth, her hands clasped white knuckled at her waist.

"Samantha, sweet, come meet your new governess."

He stopped halfway across the room but waved Miss Sasha forward. His own hands clasped white knuckled behind his back. *Please*, he begged in silence, *please be polite*.

Samantha, in all her youthful exuberance, turned to the governess with her drawing raised for admiration. "Do you like my picture?" she asked, smile never faltering when she looked up at the approaching woman.

Without hesitation, Miss Sasha accepted the offered sketch, praising it with sincerity.

"For my next picture," Samantha said, tugging at her governess' hand to join her on the floor, "I'll draw you and me sitting by the lake."

Rupert untangled his laced fingers and felt a calm within his breast. Yes, this is what they needed. A governess. Not a companion or mother. A governess. He chuckled to himself at the foolishness of love potions and chants and witches.

He chuckled to himself every evening as the trio sat by the hearth, he in his chair with a book, his daughter and Miss Sasha ensconced with drawings or games or a book of their own. He chuckled still every morning when he escorted the young ladies on a walk about the estate grounds. And during tea. And supper. And when he slipped into his bed at night. In fact, he could not recall a time when he had laughed so much or worn a smile for so long.

Samantha rarely left her new friend's side. Rupert rarely left Samantha's side. So it went every day with his gaze lingering longer on Miss Sasha's vibrant blue eye. Her half smile dispelled the shadows. Her laughter filled the rooms with music. Her witticisms charmed the staff.

One morning, Rupert maneuvered his way to her side during their morning walk, his arm offered for her to take, his other shooing Samantha ahead of them to chase the swans. He insisted Sasha share another tale of her adventures at boarding school.

The morning following, he begged for more. Again the morning after, until he could not recall a time when they had not shared their thoughts, memories, and dreams.

After one particular morning by the lake, he sought to make her smile, craved to see that heartfelt smile of hers.

"Your silence is too honest. Am I not as spellbinding a storyteller as you?" he asked when she did not laugh at the end of his tale.

Her arm tucked in the crook of his elbow, her pace in step with his, she laughed at last. "Were you trying to be funny? We really must work on your humor. You've been without companionship too long, I'm afraid, to know what makes a woman laugh," she teased.

He eyed her askance and winked.

Did she fancy him? he wondered. She had a way of looking at him when she did not think he was paying attention—a wistfulness that shone in the ocean blue of her iris.

That same evening, a full month after she had taken the position of governess, he caught his gaze resting on her profile, esteeming her. He could no longer see her scars, only the person he had come to admire. As with every evening, she sat with Samantha on her lap, the two of them reading a book together. The fire in the hearth illuminated the marred side of her face, her other half cast in shadow. Her voice rose and fell in a sing-song lyric as she read. Rupert rested his head against the chair, his eyes riveted.

She was perfect. Despite the scars. Because of the scars. With or without the scars.

A companion. A mother.

He dared not say the word *love*, but he could not deny the word tasted sweet on his lips.

Love.

The morning after, the sun rose to greet a normal day. It was not a normal day for Rupert. He paced from one side of his study to the other, waiting for Miss Sasha to arrive.

His heart raced when the door opened. One side of Sasha's bottom lip was tucked between her teeth, her hands clenched at her waist. Despite his own nervousness, he smiled to reassure her.

With a deep breath, he approached.

"I have come to admire you, Sasha, as more than a governess. I've come to think of you as a companion, as a friend." He paused when her expression dimmed. "No, strike that. Yes, as a companion and friend, but more than that. I've come to hope you might see me as more than my daughter's father. I—that is, Samantha adores you, loves you even, and I want the perfect mother for her."

He raked a hand through his hair.

"I'm bungling this." He cursed under his breath. "Let me start again. If you don't feel the same, I'll understand, but despite my best efforts to guard against these emotions, I've fallen in love with you. There. I've said it. I'm in love with you. If you would do me the honor of becoming my wife, I would see to it you know only happiness."

Although he never heard her say yes, she must have, because in the next moment, she was nestled in his arms, her lips pressed to his. A warm glow radiated through him, an indescribable pulse of heat that filled him, fulfilled him, a kind of magic that enveloped them both. He knew only love.

He leaned back to regard Sasha.

The moment shattered.

Her eyes remained closed, her lips puckered, but it was not Sasha who stood before him, rather it was Madame Esmerelda. He released her and staggered back, a hand to his heart.

There, in his study, naught but feet from him, stood the raven-haired beauty, dark and mysterious with her enticing curves.

"What is this sorcery?" he demanded to know, stepping farther away. "You've bewitched me. You've beguiled me."

The witch opened her eyes, her expression contorting into one of confusion and hurt. Shaking her head, her arms outstretched, she took a step towards him then stopped, her attention caught on the mirror above the mantel. Rapt to the reflection, she ignored

Rupert. Moving herself until she was inches away from the glass, she touched the mirror, then touched her cheek.

In a whisper not meant for him, she said, "I never thought to see this face again."

Rupert studied her every movement, her every whisper. Before him stood the witch, and yet she was not the same. The movements, the voice, the expressions — all were Sasha.

"Two years ago," said the raven-haired woman, "I visited an apothecary in search of a love potion. I wanted to find true love, you see. Men only ever wanted me for my beauty. She gave me a potion, but it all went wrong. It was a curse. The woman cursed me. She stole my face. I awoke on the fourth day, transformed into the apothecary herself."

So genuine, so guileless was Sasha that he believed her. What else was there to believe?

Rupert drew back his shoulders and admitted, "I too went to her for a love potion, but I never dreamt it would work. I sought the impossible. I sought the perfect woman. I — I sought *you*."

Collecting courage to face the impossible, he stepped behind her and clasped her shoulders, turning her towards him. Rupert searched her eyes for the truth, for any evidence of trickery, and saw within them the ocean blue eyes of his Sasha, of the woman with whom he had fallen in love. Intelligent, gentle, moral Sasha. A lost and lonely soul. A companion and a mother. The woman he loved.

In shared silence, they observed each other, learning each other anew until his laugh startled them both.

"Consider me mad," he said, tracing the curve of her chin with the pad of his thumb, "but I don't think you were cursed."

"Oh, but I was. How could it have been otherwise?"

"From my vantage point, she gave you as potent a love potion as she gave me. Don't you see? It worked."

Sasha tilted her head, her brows drawn. Then the corners of her lips lifted into a broad smile. After a hearty laugh, she wrapped her arms around his neck and sealed the spell with true love's kiss.

The Charade

April 1797

Peter,

Your most recent letter gifted me a smile that lingered for days. After sending my last, I fretted, for there are few reactions a man besotted can have to find his ladylove is intended for another. Now that the worst has been revealed, that my hand is not free, but my heart is yours, what are we to do?

Amelia

Amelia,

My initial response was what you might expect to find the woman of my heart betrothed to another, but I cannot place judgement when my situation is similar. There, I have shocked you in return. I will not speak ill of my betrothed, but suffice it to say, we do not suit. I see not why two people intended should not find cause for friendship at least, yet it would appear she and I are not destined for companionship. Unlike the two of us, two hearts entwined, two minds of understanding. I thank the Reverend Allgood for bringing us together. Can you imagine a world without our love? It is not a world in which I wish to live. If your heart is true, we will find a way.

Peter

Six months earlier

From her pew, Miss Lori Hunter quirked an eyebrow at the Reverend Allgood. A broad smile of altruistic sentiment brightened his gaunt face, wrinkled by time and goodwill.

Mr. Allgood waved a hand at the table before him, the congregation craning necks for a better look. "Here you'll find the ladies' bowl, and next to it the gentlemen's bowl. I've set out enough paper for each person to take three sheets. Come! Pick your correspondent from the bowl."

With a clap of his hands, he ushered the parishioners forward. Had he desired a tidy queue, he would have met disappointment. Lori watched, a lift at one corner of her lips, as everyone vied to be the first to take a name.

The Reverend Allgood was well-intentioned, always with a new game aimed at building camaraderie and blurring social lines. His latest was a correspondence game of charades. Into one of the bowls, each parishioner had slipped an alias. After choosing a slip of paper with the alias, the parishioner would write to their mystery correspondent with a charade to give clues to their identity. All letters were to be delivered and received at the church so as not to reveal a telltale post. Some were less than interested, but most were delighted at the chance to play a game.

As Lori approached the table, a hand cupped her elbow. When she turned, her eyes met the last man in the church she wished to see, Mr. Patrick Knowles.

With his black hair tied and bagged at the nape of his neck, a prominent Roman nose on a lean face, hazel eyes that reflected the color of his suit, and broad shoulders fitted with tailor coat, he was undeniably attractive, the most attractive of his brothers and certainly of the men in Litton. And yet Lori despised him. His sentiments mirrored hers with a sharpness about the eyes and a disapproving turn of the mouth.

"Is there something you need, Mr. Knowles?" Lori asked, her tone haughty, her words edged.

"Ensuring you're not trampled, Miss Hunter." He tugged her away from the crowd, directing her to the table. "I would be a derelict gentleman not to protect my betrothed."

Lori scoffed at his hint at manners. Mr. Knowles would not know manners if they hit him over the head. Engaged as children, a deal made between two sets of pushy parents who wished to combine neighboring lands, Mr. Knowles had devoted his childhood to tormenting her, his youth to ignoring her, and his adulthood to condescending her. He was a bore who disapproved of everything she did. Even now, she could not approach a table in a church without his eagle eye of judgement.

Tugging free, she snapped at him. "I assure you, I can walk on my own." Chin raised, she marched past him, dipped her hand in the bowl to take her slip of paper, and escaped in the opposite direction.

Only when she opened the paper did she realize she had pulled from the wrong bowl, the gentlemen's bowl. *Peter* scrawled across the paper. Oh dear. Nothing could persuade her to return the paper and face Mr. Knowles again. Her charade would need to be carefully crafted, for the game had not been intended for an improper exchange of letters between differing sexes. The excitement of such a scandal tickled her lips into a sly smile.

Good heavens, for all she knew, she could be about to write a charade for the blacksmith!

May 1797

Amelia,

For six months, we've corresponded, our letters hidden behind the church to disguise our identities. It now seems unnecessary to do so if your feelings are true. Would you feel the same to discover me a valet? A stable hand? A coachman? Would you feel shame to be on my arm at church should you discover I am too short, too tall, pock-marked, sun-kissed, too pale, too anything you may never have thought before as attractive? I do not proceed lightly, for any revelation of identity or potential union would break more hearts than our own should your love not be true. I leave you with a charade to solve. It captures my greatest fear:

My first flies on Cupid's dart.
Afflicted is my second, should we part.
A dreadful state shall be my whole
Should you forsake my soul.

Peter

Peter,

The answer to your charade is lovelorn. Do I take this to mean you fear unrequited love? Please, dear, fear not. Never have I felt this connection with another soul. I've lost count of the number of letters we've exchanged, although I've kept them all. Twice per week at least. You speak my heart's desire. You are my heart's desire. Love transcends the physical. Should you be the blacksmith – although I do hope not since Mr. Smith is already married – I would accept you as mine. You know not what I leave behind or how many hearts I will break, but to be with you, I will take the leap.

Amelia

Seated at the supper table was the Hunter family, the Knowles family, and the Popinjay family. Lori nudged the food with her fork, unable to eat. The Popinjays were boasting of their son's engagement to Miss Lydia Nibs, arranged by both parents, of course, while the Knowles and Hunters regaled all with the wedding plans between Lori and Mr. Patrick Knowles. Every time the wedding breakfast was mentioned, Lori cast a withering scowl to her intended. Rather than return her expression with one of his own, he ignored her, distracted and disinterested, not that he had ever been attentive or interested.

Her mind flitted to Peter throughout the meal. If something were to be done, it would need to be done soon, before the banns were read, a bleak and loveless future ahead. Not for the first time in six months did she wonder at Peter's identity. *Was* he a valet? Good heavens, he could be one of the footmen in this very room, exchanging one dish for another. Had Peter sorted her identity yet—a woman of means, the eldest daughter to the wealthy Hunter family, the wealthiest family in Litton, second only to the Knowles? Would he reject her with this discovery? But he knew her heart! Never could he think her pompous, spoiled, or social-minded, not when he knew *her*.

Twisting her napkin under the table, she wondered if a new note awaited her retrieval.

June 1797

Amelia,

In light of your assurance, I will reveal a hint to my profession and hope it does not come as upsetting news. Regardless of your humble origins, I accept you as you are and hope you will accept me as I am. Together, we will make a life for ourselves, away from the disapproving gaze of fellow parishioners, away from the good intentions of our relations. I have provisions saved for our needs. With this charade, you will know my profession. Tell me if with this knowledge you wish to further our plans or if the truth is undesirable:

My first describes a breeze's kiss
On whose my second is like to miss.
Combined, we doth reveal
A word to make most men kneel.

Peter

Peter,

The answer to your charade has shocked me, as you expected it would. Gentleman. You are a gentleman. This confession may shock, but it does not deter. Let us proceed as planned. But how will you feel in return to discover I may be a lady's maid or, shall I shock you further, a chambermaid?

Amelia

Lori searched the faces of the gentlemen at the soiree, the evening hosted by the Popinjays in celebration of the first of the banns being called between Mr. Paul Popinjay and Miss Lydia Nibs. Neither appeared thrilled, but the parents were elated. That would be her fate soon if Peter did not propose an elopement.

For the whole of the evening, she had studied each gentleman for clues. One of the guests must be Peter. Every gentleman in and around Litton was present tonight. How peculiar it felt, how…*exhilarating!*…to know he stood in this very room with her, hiding behind the mask of another name. Months she had spent sitting in church, eyes roaming over familiar faces, curious if he was young, old, worn, lean, rich, poor. There was, she admitted, a relief in knowing he was one of her ilk, for while jilting her intended would be shocking enough, at least she would not disgrace her family with a love match to a poverty-stricken servant. Not that she would mind as long as there was love, but the relief lightened her shoulders nonetheless.

Her gaze rested on Mr. Paul Popinjay, a youthful sort of perhaps eighteen, still pimpled, long fingers tugging at the edges of his waistcoat as his betrothed chattered in his ear. Could he be Peter? Was it disloyal to hope he was not? He did not *feel* like Peter. Surely she would recognize his spirit, his soul, his heart. Surely.

She moved her search to Mr. Laurel Knowles, her intended's younger brother by two years. He picked invisible lint from a flamboyantly embroidered coat, as handsome as all the Knowles brothers, though with a slight pudge about the middle and an air of arrogance. Her inspection shifted to Mr. Lance Knowles, the youngest brother at nineteen. His shoulder leaning against the wall, he laughed and flirted with one of Miss Nibs' aunts. Behind him stood a widowed uncle of Miss Nibs. The outside garden held his attention. Her heart skipped a beat. Could he be Peter?

The familiar grasp of her elbow interrupted her concentration. If it were not the most unladylike and most immature reaction, she would heave a sigh or roll her eyes. Instead, she beamed a friendly smile, sharp around the edges.

"Yes, Mr. Knowles?" she asked her intended with a bat of her eyelashes.

"Would you care for a lemonade?" His expression reflected her reluctance to engage in conversation.

"No, Mr. Knowles." For the first time, guilt shadowed her words.

It was not his fault he was so dreadfully dull, she supposed. Some people simply lacked spirit. However contemptuous his teasing as a youth, he had been thoughtful of late, well-meaning, even if he never engaged her in conversation, asked after her, or made any attempt to know her. Soon, she would jilt him. Yes, guilt shadowed her words.

"But thank you," she added, as though those few words would make up for the upheaval she was about to cause by eloping with Peter.

Amelia,

I could not wait another day to write to you, my love. Yesterday evening hosted a soiree. I attended, not because I enjoy soirees, but because it is what gentlemen do. Every moment, I thought of you, your hand on my arm, the two of us cutting up gaily, sharing tales and thoughts and dreams as we do in our letters. Each time I spied a maid, I questioned if she could be you. Will you not send me a happy hint as I've done for you? Be you chambermaid, lady's maid, lady, widow, or otherwise, I will cherish you always. Should your answer to my next charade be yes, meet me at the Popinjay stile in the east field at noon on Friday. I am anxious to meet and hope I do not disappoint you. From there, we may plan our escape. How will you answer this:

The self in a natural state presents my first.
The second I speak when I describe love's thirst.
United is what we shall be
If you accept my humble plea.

Peter

Peter,

Betroth is the charade's answer. A more romantic proposal I would have never dreamed! Yes, darling, yes! Your only clue to my identity is that I attended the same soiree as you. I can preempt your surprise as my quill meets paper. Now you must wonder which lady in company I might have been. I, too, searched the room for you. I had hoped my soul would find you, a connecting thread between the two of us, pulling us ever closer. Are you now questioning every woman in the room, wondering if I'm Miss Nibs' spinster aunt, Miss Hunter's youngest sister, perhaps the widowed Mrs. Moon? As you expressed, I hope I do not disappoint you. Noon on Friday.

Amelia

One hand on the stile, one hand on his heart, Patrick searched the horizon for a sign of his mystery correspondent. His pocket watch ticked a quarter past noon. Had she spied him, been disappointed, and fled?

Midges swarmed, the heat of the sun beating his brow, perspiration pooling at the base of his spine. She was not coming. For a fleeting moment, he questioned if she had ever been real or if she had been a game played by one of his younger brothers.

His heart in his throat, he propped a mud caked boot on the gate. It was best if she did not show. Too many people would be hurt by his elopement. As much as his intended did not care for him or their engagement, even she would be hurt by this, for it would be a reflection on her, a scandal from which she may not recover. For six months he had been selfish, thinking only of his own happiness to have found someone who understood him, who spoke to his heart with her own.

It was for the best his mystery love did not show. His hand had not been free to offer. Better to have a loveless marriage than to grieve his family and ruin his innocent betrothed by his leaving.

When he checked his pocket watch again, his heart thumped erratically. Half past. Mind made and spirit broken, he rounded his shoulders and turned to walk back to the Knowles' manor.

"You?" the soprano of a woman's voice questioned.

Patrick spun so quickly to meet the voice he had to reach for the fence to steady himself. Before him stood his intended Miss Lori Hunter, her brow furrowed and her eyes wide. In the space of a few seconds, he panicked at being caught by Miss Hunter — *anyone but her!* — while meeting his mystery love. Then all at once, it hit him. He tightened his grip on the fence.

"You?" he echoed.

Miss Hunter looked about them before training her cerulean blue eyes on him. "Did…did someone send you?" she asked.

Not knowing if he should laugh or cry, he settled for a smile, somewhere between coy and bashful. "If you wish to pretend to be a messenger for Miss Amelia, bringing an apology to Mr. Peter, then I'll understand. If, on the other hand, you'll accept me, I'm here as my own messenger, a lovesick Peter head over boots for a woman who prefers watercolors to embroidery, longs for the smell of the ocean on a moonlit night, and dreams of the rumbling voice of a gentleman reading Donne by the fireside. What do you think, Miss Hunter? Are you a messenger? Or are you my love?"

Her mouth trembled, and her eyes watered. When her body swayed forward as though to swoon, Patrick reached out to catch her only to find her already in his arms, her hands framing his face and her lips greeting his.

She leaned back, her lips still parted from their kiss. "If you can solve this charade, you'll have my answer:

My first is the means of sight.

My second inspires poets to write.

My third bleats herself to sleep.

United we reflect emotions deep."

Patrick threw back his head in a laugh and twirled his betrothed. "Too easy. Eye love ewe, too, my sweet."

With words of affection exchanged, they renewed their promises with another kiss.

The Return

Frederick stared at the door to *The Swan and Crown*. He knew when he opened the door, the hinges would creak. He knew when he stepped inside the taproom, the scent of ale would assault his nostrils. He knew when he walked up the stairs to the assembly rooms, familiar faces would line with smiles.

The nostalgia accompanying his return surprised him. Familiarity of sights was expected, but it was the scents and sounds that moved him the most, that brought a sense of homecoming to drive the hardest man to tears. The lavender of his mother. The camphor of his father. The loam of the family wolfhound.

Even the exchange of money for manor carried a scent, nostalgia eddying before flowing into a future of his own current, the scent mossy. Once the abandoned manor had been a dream home, a playground for idle children. Now it was the harbinger of happiness. It awaited renovation, laughter, and a bride.

Frederick stared at the door to *The Swan and Crown*.

Would she still remind him of an Easter sunrise? Heart in his throat, he opened the door. The hinges creaked. The ale assailed. The faces smiled. Five years was a long time to absent oneself, living in a foreign country to earn wealth. Would she still remind him of the Twelfth Night?

A self-made gentleman, he stepped into the ball-room. Friends and fellow villagers greeted him, all smiles and handshakes. A few knowing eyes wandered to the dancefloor, flitting between Frederick and the figures.

Hands guided him down the two-row queue of familiar faces, each pat to the back inching him closer to the dancers. Thirsty eyes searched one couple after another, parched for a glimpse of her, just one to reassure himself she had not changed.

There, between the soldier and the vicar. A glimpse.

A shimmer of pink and ebony twirled out of sight. Frederick arched his neck, craning for another glimpse.

There, hands clasped with the widow Jenkins and Lady Penelope. A glimpse.

A chime of laughter echoed out of hearing. Frederick rocked onto the balls of his feet, gleaning for a fragment of her.

There, fingers on the sleeve of his childhood friend. Her face was aglow with happiness and upturned to admire her dance partner as they promenaded.

Frederick's heart thumped to a halt. All he had done had been for her, for them, for their future happiness. Five years had been too long for her. He read it in her features, in the attention she focused on the other man. All he had done had been for nothing.

Head bowed, he turned to the door.

"Frederick!" cried a voice of silk behind him.

He turned back to the dancefloor. The music stopped; the figures slowed; the crowd parted. Leaving her dance partner behind, Corinne dashed across the ballroom and embraced Frederick with arms scented of jasmine.

The villagers forgotten, Frederick enfolded Corinne, inhaling the scent of past infusing future, their past transmuting into their future.

The Marriage

The none-too-gentle sway of the carriage lulled Francine's mother into slumber, the woman's chin resting against her chest as her head bobbed in time with the bumps in the road. Franny could not imagine sleeping. Not when they would soon arrive at the estate. Not when she knew *he* would be waiting for her.

One year and three days had not dulled her heartache.

Not a half hour after her mother's snores brought a smile to Franny's lips did the carriage pass the gatehouse. Nose pressed to window, she watched as moors gave way to lawn. Had he arrived before her? Would she have a moment to refresh before seeing him? She knew he would attend her stepbrother's wedding breakfast at the end of the week. He had written to say as much. An impersonal letter no more than a few lines, lines she had traced with her fingertips a dozen times before folding the letter and tucking it into the escritoire cubby.

Cresting a hill, the carriage overlooked the park. The estate rose into view on the next peak, majestic, situated to catch the admiration of approaching callers. Franny's heart raced at the sight of the Palladian mansion. Five years of happiness she experienced at her stepfather's home, then eight months of unhappiness after her stepbrother inherited. She had not seen it in one year and three days. Not the estate. Not her stepbrother. Not *him*.

The carriage descended the other side of the hill, the estate drifting out of view. Franny nudged her mother awake before setting about tying her bonnet and smoothing out her dress.

When the estate came into view once more, it was not the stone visage that caught Franny's attention, but the figure standing watch in the circle drive. Squint as she might, she could not make out the face. The set of the shoulders and the stance of the hips told her what she needed to know. She leaned her head against the carriage seat, closing her eyes in silent prayer to still her trembling limbs, to steady the quiver in her voice, and to mask emotion.

The vehicle slowed to a stop. Horse snorts and grooms' voices could not overpower the crunch of gravel underfoot, a steady gait of approaching man. With a deep breath and a nod to her mother, Franny turned to the carriage door as it opened to a waiting hand.

Her first sight of him dizzied her senses. He had not changed except the silvering at his temples. One year and three days.

"Mr. Hamlin," she greeted him, her smile broad, her eyes searching.

He pressed his lips to her gloved knuckles, his gaze meeting hers. "Mrs. Hamlin."

And with that, he turned his attention to her mother.

Oh, Bertrand.

Not until dinner, the other guests having arrived throughout the day, did she see her husband again. They were seated together at the table, forced into conversation by proximity. She could hardly eat a bite.

What she wanted to say — *I've loved you for seven years* — was a far cry from what she said — *Lindenford Hall is lovely this time of year*. That he had to ask after his own home chipped at her heart. Why had he married her if he did not want to live with her at Lindenford?

Oh, yes, of course, the dowry.

Best not allow reality to intrude. She had not seen him since the wedding day, since an hour after their own wedding breakfast, as a matter of fact, and she wanted to make the most of her time with him now. How funny was fate that when they parted at the end of the week, it would yet again be at a wedding breakfast?

Although now only eight and thirty, Bertrand had once been her stepfather's closest friend. Franny first met him at a dinner party in that very dining room, she sixteen, he one and thirty. With each year and each of his visits to the estate, her love for him grew, though he never noticed her. How could she have declined his proposal when he came to her those many months after her stepfather's death? However sudden, however unexpected, she never could have said no to him. That he sent her and her mother to his home without consummating the marriage, without even joining them for the journey, revealed his true reason for marrying her — the money — but that truth had not soured her affection for him.

Did he still see her as the silly girl of her youth?

Dinner left Franny giddy at the familiar lilt of his voice, the sapphire of his eyes, and the scent of his shaving soap, musky with a hint of leather and cloves. And yet she could not sleep from how bereft the conversation left her, an exchange of empty words. That they shared the suite kept her awake longer than the shallow conversation. Rather than her old bedroom, she had been given one of the suites. Two guest rooms connected via a small parlor, on one side of the parlor, Bertie's room. Did he, too, stand at the connecting door, a hand to the wood, imagining the person on the other side?

The next day, she roamed the rose garden, the vines and bushes in full May bloom. Footsteps on the stone path behind her caught her attention. She turned. Her heart thumped erratically at the sight of him. Beneath the arched entrance, Bertrand stood, his brows drawn in thought, his step hesitant, his eyes locked with hers.

"Am I disturbing you?" he asked.

Grasping the chance, she said a tad too hurriedly, "No, please, I welcome your company."

An expression crossed his features, gone before she could read it. Pleasure? Surprise? Or had that been what she wanted to read in his face?

His features a mask, he approached. "If you'll pardon my bluntness, I'm happy to see you. Many a time I've wanted to ride out to Lindenford, to ascertain your comfort, but I never wanted to disturb you or press my company. You've taken to the new mare I sent?"

Franny patted to one side of the stone bench for him to join her. He did. The waft of that heavenly scent butterflied her heart down through her abdomen.

"Yes, thank you for Juno. She's divine." Tentative, she looked at him askance from beneath her eyelashes. "I wish you would come to the hall. I've never seen it through your eyes."

Was that too bold? Did the words make her sound that silly child of old?

Bertie angled himself on the bench, studying her with a crease between his brows. "I want you to feel free to live your life, Mrs. Hamlin, without me hanging over your shoulder."

His words lingered throughout the day and on into dinner, where they shared another polite conversation. When she spent another sleepless night standing at the connecting door, her palm to the wood, her cheek against the cold grain, she wondered at his meaning.

On the third day, she took in the rose garden once more. And once more, Bertrand appeared in the arched entry, dashing in a cobalt suit, and wishing not to disturb her but desiring a moment of her time.

His hands, strong with long fingers, clasped in his lap as he said to the stone underfoot, "Have you made friends? I hoped you might favor the Lovells. Their daughter is near your age, as is their—" His voice caught on the final word. "Son."

Franny moved her hand to lie between them, palm up in invitation. "Yes, they're a lovely family. As are the Janes. I'm enamored with Mrs. Janes' youngest. Such a mischievous little boy."

Bertie did not take her hand as she hoped. He spoke few words, the conversation stilted. That he made the effort meant enough. Had he not made the effort, she would have been certain he regretted marrying her, saddled with a woman he did not desire.

That evening, they shared a settee in the drawing room while Franny's future sister-in-law delighted the guests with a song at the pianoforte. A time or two, their legs brushed. The touch thrilled Franny, tingling her flesh and fluttering her heart.

Another sleepless night of cheek to door. No, not an entirely sleepless night. At some point, perhaps near midnight, Franny awoke in the shared parlor, curled in a chair facing his door. She must have drifted off while keeping vigil. What startled her awake was not the realization she was still in the parlor but the blanket that wrapped around her and the warmth of a freshly stoked fire. Staring at his closed door, she cocked her head. The blanket smelled of him, deliciously of him.

The fourth day of her stay, two days before the wedding breakfast, found her in the rose garden at the same time as the previous days. This time, she sat poised on the bench, eyes trained on the arch. Like clockwork, Bertrand stepped into the garden, his expression curious and, if she read it correctly, hopeful, though she knew not what he hoped.

"Sit with me?" Franny patted the bench.

"I don't wish to disturb you," he confessed as he accepted the invitation and sat next to her.

"Your company is why I came here today. And while I'm being honest, it's why I accepted the invitation to the wedding breakfast."

His perplexed expression spurred her to continue, though she worried only heartache waited at the end of her words.

"It may sound heartless of me," she said, "but I care not for my stepbrother's nuptials. What I do care about is you. I know you married me for the dowry, but that does not mean we can't make a real marriage of this arrangement." Her heart pounded in her ears.

Bertie turned fully to face her. His features clouded, but his eyes brightened. "Francine, you had no dowry."

She clenched her fists to her waist. "Of course, I did. Twenty thousand. It's why you married me."

He shook his head. "Your brother spent the dowry in the first month of his inheritance. With nothing in writing, the money was his to do with as he willed. I couldn't bear to see you unhappy or passed on to one of his friends. I married you to free you. I wanted you to have the security of my name and never want for wealth."

The words shocked her to her core. There had been no dowry. He had not married her for the money.

Searching his eyes for answers, she asked, "Is that the only reason you married me?"

He turned away.

Franny's mind was in turmoil. One year and three days she had thought the man she loved married her for money, but now, now what was she to think?

When he did not answer, she said, "I'm a silly girl to you. Aren't I? You felt sorry for me and so gave me your name. You have your steward spoil me with gifts, but you never desire my company. I've loved you for seven years, and all you see is your friend's tittering stepdaughter."

He whipped around to face her. "What did you say?"

Startled by his ferocious frown, she hesitated in her reply. "You think me too young, never mind that I'm past my majority."

"No, not that part." He slipped a hand in the vee of his waistcoat, rubbing his chest just over his heart. "You said you've loved me for seven years."

Franny nodded, looking down at her hands, knuckles white with tension. "Now you can think me even sillier. The happiest moment of my life was when we exchanged vows. I thought…I thought you loved me, too. But then you left."

"Good God, Francine." Clasping her hand in his, he leaned in to press her palm over his heart. "I thought you desired freedom from your stepbrother. Sacrificing yourself to an older man for whom you cared nothing was worth the escape. I gave you what I thought you wanted — freedom. I thought you might find love yet if I stepped aside, giving you the only things I knew to give."

Wrapping her mind around his words shivered her body. She began to tremble and could not stop. A warm May day, and she shook as though from a chill. In a flash, his arms came around her, and he pulled her into his embrace. She buried her face into the folds of his cravat and inhaled the cologne of cloves, releasing all her tension against the hard planes of his chest. His arms tightened, his nose nuzzling her temple.

In a rasping voice, he said, "You can't know how much or for how long I've loved you."

She leaned back to look into his eyes, her hands snaking up his chest to frame his face. "As I've loved you."

His lips found hers, their first kiss in a lifetime of love.

Guest Authors

Love At Rescue

A Bramley Hall Regency Romance

By Michelle Helen Fritz & E.A. Shanniak

"Good Heavens, sir!" Miss Purcellville exclaimed. Simon felt heat creep into his cheeks as curious gazes and gasping at the frightening scene that had just occurred, drew unwanted attention. It took Simon a few moments to untangle their limbs from the lady's cloak. Once gaining his feet, Simon bent down, helping the beautifully unsettled woman rise to her feet.

The lady glared at him, holding a crumpled letter in her hands. He paused mid-motion wondering if he should help dust her off or if it would add to their precarious moment. The woman blinked at him, trying to fix her bonnet and auburn ringlets that were in disarray. Her reticule was discarded in the grass near her slippered feet. Simon bent down, retrieving it and offered it back to its owner.

"Are you all right?" he inquired softly.

Simon took a step away for propriety's sake, admiring the pink hue in her cheeks and the curls of her auburn hair peeking out from beneath her bonnet. Long dark lashes batted angrily at him. He spied the chocolate color of her eyes, flecked with hints of gold from under the glare, and pout of her full lips.

The lady was nearly trampled by a runaway horse and carriage. She was so absorbed in her letter, she didn't hear the bellowing of the carriage driver nor the frightened shrieks of passersby dashing to the side of the road for safety. Forgoing all civility, he dashed to secure her life; only to land on the manicured city garden, covered in stains and flower petals. Unfortunately, by saving her, it put them in quite the scandalous predicament.

"I say, Mr. Morten, thank you for saving my daughter's life," Lord Purcellville boomed, breathing heavily as he came to his daughter's aid. "Dearest Alicia, my sweet girl, are you all right?"

"Yes Papa," Miss. Purcellville replied, removing the glower from her brow. "What was all the fuss over?"

"Do you not recall?"

Miss Purcellville shook her head. "No, I do not. I was completely absorbed in my letter."

Lord Purcellville turned, motioning to him. "Mr. Morten saved your life."

Miss. Purcellville's cream-colored face paled slightly. She immediately dipped her head and went into a curtsey. Simon bowed in return, feeling the heat return to his cheeks. He was not some green lad, yet he found he could not help but to degenerate within her presence. It was most unmanning and his natural confidence was wanning. Miss. Purcellville was a magnificent creature with a voice that could put the angels of the heavens to shame.

"Thank you, Mr. Morten, I am forever grateful," she said.

The softness in her voice coupled with the sparkle in her eyes left him entirely speechless. How could he begin to formulate a response when a goddess stood before him?

Simon shook his head and softly cleared his throat. "The pleasure is all mine, I assure you."

Lord Purcellville grasped his daughter's hand, folding it into the crook of his arm. "Simon, could you please accompany me back into my study, there is something which we need to discuss."

"Yes, Lord Purcellville," Simon replied with a bow.

Simon followed in step, slightly behind the lord and his daughter. He swallowed, wondering if he was going to be reprimanded and be given duties for disobedience. Simon pulled at the collar around his neck, watching his booted feet and the ground pass him by.

Glancing up, the marble columns of the Purcellville estate greeted his gaze. Potted plants with evergreen shrubs mingling with golden flowers were placed on either side of the columns adding elegance and a cozy, welcoming feeling. The butler opened the double polished oaken doors for Miss. Purcellville and she entered, calling for her beloved mama.

"Simon," Lord Purcellville called from the cusp of the entryway, "please follow me to the study."

Simon nodded his understanding, feeling this throat become parched at the cold air surrounding him. He followed the distinguished lord into his study. Lord Purcellville took his seat and motioned for Simon to take his. His blood ran hot under his skin, wondering at what kind of reprimand he would receive. Lord Purcellville was an excellent yet strict commander of the King's Armies. To make the situation more precarious, the way he had tumbled in his plight to save the woman made it look to the ton a bit more than just saving a damsel in distress. He wondered briefly if this would be an act of chivalry gone terribly wrong.

"Thank you again Simon for saving my daughter's life," Lord Purcellville stated as he leaned back in his desk chair.

Simon forced his hands to stay in his lap instead of rubbing the clammy nerves off on his pressed regiment issued pants. "'Tis an honor I shall cherish forever."

The man nodded, a grin creeping across his face. Simon slowly closed his eyes, wondering what he would have to do. Certainly mucking stalls or shining boots was a fitting punishment? Surely this good deed wouldn't land him in disbandonment from the regiment, dishonoring his family name?

"In appreciation, I would like to bestow you with my finest hunting hound, what say you?" inquired his lordship.

Shocked, Simon replied, "I'm sorry?"

"Of course, if you would rather, you may have my daughter's hand in marriage.

Alicia is beautiful, is she not?"

Simon nodded. "Absolutely breathtaking." Simon swallowed. Was this great man jesting with him? The strict face of Lord Purcellville crumbled slightly at the corner of his lips. Simon felt a bead of sweat trickle down his back.

"I have a proposition for you Mr. Morten," the lord began, leaning back in his chair. "My daughter is quite smitten with you. So, you can either court my daughter or have my finest hound."

Simon blinked, finding himself stuttering for words. "Your answer, my boy," Lord Purcellville prompted.

"I would be honored to court your daughter as I have no need for a hound."

Top Hats and Tails

By C.A. Leighton

I t was not supposed to be this way.

Gavin looked to the north. To the south. Left and right. The crossroads rose as an island in a sea of mist in a world of grey.

Tavish swore as he tossed his top hat to the ground. He glared as he spoke, "we'll never make it. We should have taken auntie's motor."

Stooping swoop, Gavin rescued the discarded headwear. Fixing the brim, he spoke with nonchalance, "oh aye, and why's that then?"

Grumbling, Tavish kicked the ground as he snatched the proffered hat, "because the Jaguar is faster than your Rover."

To this Gavin could not help but grin, although he corrected, "it's not faster, lad, it's just your aunt disregards speed postings."

Not wanting to hear this, Tavish clenched his hands and failed to contain an internal scream. Then he retorted, "at least it runs."

No one but Tavish witnessed the frost of Gavin's gaze.

Clearing his throat, Gavin prompted, "if you're done, the McGuffins live this way. We can best make plans there."

With reluctance, Tavish fell in step beside his uncle.

As they trudged up the gravel lane, Tavish pondered allowed, "didn't you sell the McGuffins some of your horses?"

Gavin nodded. In the paddock, a herd of horses could be seen in the clear patches of the wispy mist. Majestic creatures.

Continuing toward the stacked stone farmhouse, Gavin noticed Tavish peering round.

Straightening, Tavish crossed his arms, "where's their motor?"

"They don't have one," Gavin let that sink in, "don't worry lad, we'll get there."

Gavin had promised his nephew he would get him to the church on time. They both cut fine figures astride the Clydesdales. The beaming smile on the bride's face spoke of a day not soon forgotten.

The Choice

By H. J. Palmer

M y heart had stopped, and for a second—just a second, mind you—I felt like I was plummeting. Then my grandmother took my arm and my heart started again. I took a deep breath, trying to sweep away my nerves from her all-seeing eyes.

She gave me a small smile. "All will be well, young bride."

At the title, Fear and Doubt whispered into my mind. *"What if you do not like him?"* Fear said.

"What if he does not like you?" Doubt retorted.

"What if he is abusive?"

"Or ugly?"

"Or cruel"

"Or—"

"Stop fretting, Maria. Your fiancé is a man of honour. That is what makes a marriage," she patted my hand, propelling me to view my reflection in a bucket of water. I was the most beautiful that I had ever been. But my fear was also at its peak, making my reflection wane."

"Let me pause for a moment, my love, to reassure you. I wanted a husband, a protector, a lover," Maria waggled her eyebrows as her own granddaughter's face reddened, "children, and grandchildren. I wanted you, Atoni. But I feared how the match would go. I needn't have."

"Attendants swirled around me, making preparations that I would never remember. All I knew was the question: Had my grandmother chosen my husband well? I blinked and I was at the wedding. Emotion flooded me, and I wasn't sure if I could do it.

Then I saw him. Let me tell you he was the most handsome man I had ever seen! I dragged my poor grandmother up the aisle in half a second so that I could get a closer look. He was even more gorgeous up close, but the best part of him was his eyes. He had such kind eyes.

I remember my grandmother laughing, his wide smile, the buzz when he took my hand, and his quiet jokes to put me at ease. Time flew under our elation.

The next moment we were in the bedchamber," Maria smirked at Atoni's equal mortification and intrigue, "and yes, there was embarrassment, pain, and fear. There was also love, passion, and pleasure. Suffice to say we learnt together. All things are achievable with time.

He took a week just to be with me, and it was divine. Passions ran high and we fought a lot - and loved a lot, too. I could barely stand the thought of going to sleep, I missed him so.

I was heartbroken when he returned to his duties. Oh, how I missed him those long days as he ploughed the fields! Not for long though, as I soon learnt that I had a child to prepare for."

"My mother," said Atoni.

Maria nodded. "Your mother. The years passed in a haze of love, work, and happiness. Your uncles and aunts were born, as we worked, loved, raised our children, and even mourned, as one. Many seasons came and passed. When your mother came of age, she chose to pursue a life with marriage and children. My mother found your mother a husband, with whom she has been happy for many years. Can you fault your father?"

Atoni shook her head reluctantly.

"Then they bore my greatest joy - you. So you see, though I did not know your grandfather before our wedding day, because we worked hard on our marriage, breaking and compromising, forgiving and changing, growing *together*, we are happy. Love begets love. I now know that my grandmother was right; honourable men make for good husbands. You have chosen to be a wife. And I have chosen for you a man of honour. Atoni, you will have many a happy year with him. Trust me, my love. Am I not wise? Do I not know you well? Do I not understand marriage?"

Atoni hung her head. "I am sure you have made the right choice, grandmother." Her tone was that of doubtful youth.

Maria smiled, knowing that her story had failed to allay her granddaughter's fears. She knew, too, that Atoni had an additional fear of those that were her own all those years ago. Atoni was deeply in love with a young man in their village. Could she give him up to have the family that she wanted?

Come tomorrow, Atoni would discover him waiting for her at the altar. The life that followed would be filled with love.

Henri

By Carla Jo Pimentel

Penelope Peabody was not at all what Henrietta expected. She thought she would meet a spoiled, rich brat, but instead she was met by the sweetest, most genuine teenager she had ever met. She reminded Henri of herself at that age. A girl who could shine but preferred to stay in the background.

That was the challenge, convincing Penelope that she was spectacular. Penelope didn't want anything to do with the party. She could not understand why her brother wanted to put her in the spotlight. Between Penelope's hesitation and only having a few months to prepare, Henri had to work overtime to ensure it was a success. She was determined to make it enjoyable for Penelope. That was her goal, and she was willing to do whatever it took.

Having been working with the Peabody's for a couple of months, she felt stressed but knew it would be worth it in the end. She had heard horrible comments regarding Mr. Peabody and she was glad he had not made an appearance. That was one man she didn't look forward to meeting! She had heard he hated women, so her perception of him was not a positive one. Sean, Forsyth Peabody's assistant, assured her that he would not have time to time to even look her way at the party, and she was more than thankful for that! Forsyth Peabody was one man she did not wish to encounter!

"Miss Woods, I don't like to be the center of attention," Penelope complained.

"How will I ever wear heels? To be honest, I don't even have a lot of friends. Most of the guests will be my family's friends and business associates. Why am I being subjected to this?"

Henri felt for her. She had been a wallflower too. Oh, but if she only knew her worth! If she could help Penelope gain at least a little confidence, she would consider it a job well done. Not only would Penelope have a magnificent party, but it would be on her terms. It was all about compromise.

One evening, as Henri was wrapping up for the night, a man she had not seen before walked in. He walked over to her admiring the ballroom.

"Hello, I'm FJ. I was told about this beautiful set up you have here and had to see it for myself. Do you mind if I just look around?"

"Not at all. Make yourself at home. I'm just finishing up," she responded as she wondered who this FJ person was. He was a tall, simple looking man. With kind green eyes and salt and pepper hair he looked to be in his mid 30s. He wore ripped jeans and a t-shirt, nothing special, but there was something about him that intrigued her.

She left him so he could look around on his own. The party would be in a few days and although the finishing touches were pending, it was breathtaking.

Henri was proud and ecstatic because Penelope was getting the party she wanted. And that's how it should be right? You only turn sixteen once. They had compromised on a few details, well maybe on a lot, but the outcome was pleasing to both.

The ballroom was decorated in black and gold. Pulling off decorations in those colors had been a task, but she did it. All the details portrayed her hard labor. The flowers were small and delicate, like Penelope wanted, nothing elaborate or gaudy, just simple and elegant.

"The place is stunning, Miss Woods. I am certain everyone will agree with me in saying that you have outdone yourself."

"Call me Henri. I appreciate your input. This has been one of my biggest challenges, but Penelope is ecstatic, so my work is done," she answered with a big smile.

"How did you do it? She didn't even want a party to begin with and now she can't stop talking about it."

"I just listened to her. She's a wonderful girl."

"That she is. I appreciate you allowing me to look around."

"No problem. Have a goodnight, FJ!"

"Hopefully, I will see you again, Henri."

Penelope's sweet sixteen was a big hit! She wore a beautiful gold gown, long and exquisite but unpretentious, just like she wanted. And she wore her black Converse. No one knew and she was comfortable without the agony of heels.

From afar, Henrietta noticed a man who looked vaguely familiar. He caught her looking and walked over immediately. It was FJ! He sure did clean up nicely! Suddenly, she felt nervous.

"Hello, Henri! This has been quite a successful gathering."

"Thank you. I didn't expect to see you here," she blurted out.

"You didn't? I would not miss my sister's sweet sixteen for the world!"

"Your sister?" This was Forsyth Peabody? How was that even possible? He was so kind, with eyes that could melt any woman's heart.

"You said your name is FJ."

"Yes, I go by FJ. It's less intimidating. I don't know why but people seem scared of me, especially women. I can't figure it out. My mother says it's because I don't seem approachable and barely talk to anyone, but I'm a little timid. Being here tonight has really drained my social battery. But I was looking forward to seeing you again."

She could not believe that Forsyth Peabody was this gentle, warm-hearted man, proving that sometimes things are not what they seem. All fears she'd had about meeting this man dissipated when he smiled.

"You look beautiful, Henri. Would you like to dance?"

She took his hand and allowed him to lead her to the dance floor. They danced all night, knowing this was just the beginning.

A Note from Paullett Golden

Dear Reader,

Thank you for reading this collection of short fiction. If you're interested in learning more about the authors featured in this book, read their bios in the next few pages and follow their provided social accounts where applicable.

This collection offered flash and short fiction exclusively. If you're interested in exploring this type of fiction further, check out my blog: https://www.paullettgolden.com/post/flash-fiction-writing

Supporting indie writers who brave self-publishing is important and appreciated. I humbly request you review this book on Amazon with an honest opinion. Reviewing elsewhere is additionally much appreciated.

One way to support writers you've enjoyed reading, indie or otherwise, is to share their work with friends, family, book clubs, etc. Lend books, share books, exchange books, recommend books, and gift books. If you especially enjoyed a writer's book, lend it to someone to read in case they might find a new favorite author in the book you've shared.

All the best,
Paullett Golden

About Paullett Golden

Celebrated for her complex characters, realistic conflicts, and sensual portrayal of love, Paullett Golden writes historical romance for intellectuals. Her novels, set primarily in Georgian England, challenge the genre's norm by starring characters loved for their flaws, imperfections, and idiosyncrasies. Her plots explore human psyche, mental and physical trauma, and personal convictions. Her stories show love overcoming adversity. Whatever our self-doubts, *love will out*.

Connect online
paullettgolden.com
facebook.com/paullettgolden
twitter.com/paullettgolden
instagram.com/paullettgolden

About Michelle Helen Fritz

Michelle Helen Fritz loves to write about dashing heroes and the compelling women that tempt them with a dash of intrigue, an abundant amount of romance, and scenes that hopefully make her readers swoon. She is the mother of four children whom she homeschools and currently resides in Maryland with her own jaunty hero who makes all of her dreams come true.

Connect online
facebook.com/Author-Michelle-Helen-Fritz-111085181423828
instagram.com/authormichellehelenfritz

About C.A. Leighton

C.A. Leighton is most at home on a yoga mat or exploring outdoors hiking. Her writing passion lies in world building and mythos research, preferring to combine fantasy genre elements of sci-fi, Greek mythology and epic poetry, mixing in a dose of steampunk vibes for good measure. Ever curious about origins of words, etymology is another hobby. Her passion in art is in digital portraits and large canvas paintings of flowers.

About H.J. Palmer

Hannah is twenty-four and lives in regional NSW, Australia. She lives with her husband and their two sons (both under four) and the family's pet dog, Rocky. When she is not wiping a bum or being overwhelmed by testosterone, Hannah is working on her novels and reading anything that she can get her hands on. She attributes all credit to God, coffee, and her husband, who kindly watches the kids while she writes.

About Carla Jo Pimentel

Carla Jo Pimentel is married, has three children, three grandchildren and two dogs. To say she is busy is an understatement but she makes time for what matters most. She credits her resilience and strength to her faith and relationship to God. Her greatest pleasure comes from spending time with her family, but she also enjoys reading, writing, having tea with friends, traveling, listening to music, and dancing, even if it's just in her living room.

Carla has been teaching freshman English for a few years and is passionate about instilling a greater appreciation for the written word in all her students. She writes entertaining stories for all ages and stages and will be releasing her first children's book, *Francesca the Unicorn*, later this year. Her other stories will follow as she is working on the final touches.

Connect online
carlajopimentel.com
facebook.com/Carla-Jo-Pimentel-106473591653872

About E.A. Shanniak

E.A. (Ericka) Shanniak is a multi-genre romance author from a small town in South Central, Kansas. When not working, she fishes, dirt bikes and voraciously reads. She is a mom of 2 kids, and a pretty chill wife. You can follow her on Facebook and Instagram. Be sure to check out her group shanniak shenanigans for the latest news, releases and giveaways.

Connect online
facebook.com/eashanniakromance
instagram.com/author_ea.shanniak